STONE

Jan Michael, born in the Yorkshire Dales, has lived much of her life abroad, eventually returning to the U.K., to live and work in Settle where this story is mainly set. She has had fourteen novels published, some for adults, others for children. Many have been translated, into, variously, Dutch, German, Japanese, Italian, Polish and Danish; two were turned into operas.

Praise for books by the same author:

'An atmospheric, unusual novel,' *The Guardian* of *Hill of Darkness*

'The honest, nuanced and optimistic portrait of an unusual individual.' *Vrij Nederland* of *A Cluster of Camphire*

'A touching and fascinating tale of a love turned by art to stone. Compelling and vivid.' Emma Tennant of *The Lost Lover*

'The newcomer is sharply observed with a mixture of dislike and affection; the story is seductively extreme… the same radical naivety characterises *Flying Crooked*.' *De Groene Amsterdammer* of *Amsterdam Blues* and *Flying Crooked*

'A celebration of life in all its prosaic glory.' *Vancouver Sun* of *Flying Crooked*

STONE ON STONE

JAN MICHAEL

G
Gabriel Press

First published in Great Britain in 2016

By Gabriel Press

9 Lower Croft Street, Settle, North Yorkshire BD24 9HH

www.jan-michael.co.uk

British Library Cataloguing in Publication Data available
ISBN 978-0-9576533-1-3

Cover design Chris Burgon
Photograph Paul Clark

Printed and bound in Great Britain by

Lamberts Print & Design

2 Station Road, Settle, North Yorkshire BD24 9AA

In memory of Elizabeth and Iori

For Mari, with love

'Lighten our darkness, we beseech thee, O Lord, and by thy great mercy defend us from all perils and dangers of this night.'

Book of Common Prayer

'I had my dream last night. I'm in a city, trying to go home. Everyone is kind. I stop, and people come up and ask me where I want to go. Suddenly I'm in another street and walking, and people still come up and ask me. Everyone is helpful. But the trouble is, I don't know where I want to go; I don't know the house, I don't even know the road.'

One

'I've decided to leave my body to the nearest medical school when I'm dead. To be chopped up and prodded, I mean - not for transplants. Watch out! You're dripping coffee all over my toast.'

Ben banged down the coffee pot, his wrist suddenly weak.

'You almost cracked the table,' Maryann reproached him.

Ben didn't care. They'd bought it in a fit of enthusiasm fifteen years before and not got around to shedding it; they should, its glass top was too cold to the touch. He didn't want his coffee now. 'What are you trying to tell me?'

'Just exactly what I have told you.' Catlike, she licked a blob of curd from the corner of her mouth. 'I've decided to leave-'

'All right, all right. I heard you the first time.'

'Well then.'

'Are you planning on dying, I mean, in the near

future?' Ben tried to keep his voice light, but his body betrayed him as one hand pushed his plate away. He liked breakfast, usually. 'I mean, are you trying to tell me that you're ill? Maryann? Are you?'

She crunched toast, regarding him steadily. Her eyes, slanting and green, had reduced him to putty when they were newly together, and sometimes still. Not at this moment. She put down her toast and took his hand. 'You're cold.'

'It's the blasted table.'

'We'll get rid of it. Now. Today.'

'You're not answering my question. Are you ill?'

'Of course I'm not. I'd have told you if I were.'

'Would you? Would you really?'

'Of course I would.'

'Of course you would. What about the time you bought a bed when I was away?'

'It was a *present!*' She looked bemused. 'And you liked it.'

'It was a fait accompli.'

'Oh, don't be cross.'

'I'm not cross.'

'You are. Listen to you. And your hands are shaking.'

'No wonder. Leaving your body to a medical school. I love your body. I love you.'

'And I love you. And your body. But when I'm gone, my body will be gone.' She smoothed down the obstinate bit of his hair at the front that she called his cock's crest.

'Oh!' He batted away her hand. She was at her most infuriating. 'I'm going to my studio. And you,' he pointed a teaspoon at her, 'had better be here when I'm back later. And not lying on the floor dead!'

The studio wasn't exactly far, just out of the kitchen door, past a soggy patch of mint and watercress and the pits from when the house had been a thriving tannery. Each day Ben went to the studio, Maryann to her work as archivist in Chapel Street; they rarely met for lunch.

The studio was a mess. The drawers in the old apothecary chest hung open from his hunt for a ruler the day before; there were dead flies on the windowsill, and dust, and he'd not thrown away the dirty painting water the previous evening because of wanting to get out for a drink with Maryann. He could try tidying it; it'd give him something practical to do. But he wanted to get on with painting, too. His blood was fizzing as if he was high on caffeine.

No, he wouldn't tidy; he would paint. He stood at his high table, brushed his arm over the thick paper waiting there. It would be like her, not really telling him some awful truth. No, that wasn't fair; they had their ways of coping with each other, and she did sometimes hold things back as if waiting for the moment that he could take them in, accept them.

He couldn't settle. He threw down the brush that was in his hand. It spattered blue where he hadn't wanted on the blank paper, ruining it. He scrunched it up and dropped it on the floor, and hurried back to the house to pick up his phone from where he'd left it on the kitchen table. He pressed in her number. Voicemail. 'Ring me,' he said. He stood, irresolute.

Only one thing might ease his jumpiness. Leaving the phone behind, in contradiction to his message, he tugged on walking boots and went out and up the moor, higher, always higher, forced-march pace, till the way levelled out. A lark above kept him company, sheep and cows grazed at his side, sun struck him intermittently through clouds; he registered none as he headed for the foss, a haunt since boyhood. Down through the dell, on a rock, he unlaced his boots and scrambled his slippery way to reach the pool where he stripped off and dived in, swimming for the waterfall then turning his back on it. It swamped his head and shoulders, roared into his ears, blinded his eyes, pounded him back to an even keel. Calm at last, he swam round the peaty pool, a goldfish in its bowl, then flipped onto his back to gaze up at the canopy of leaves that caught the sun above. A pity Maryann wasn't with him; she enjoyed it here just as much. His crossness had ebbed away and now he was just surprised at his over-reaction. He'd be able to discuss it better with her that evening; they'd sort it out fine.

Two

'How lovely.' Maryann came outside, slipping off her shoes, running fingers through her hair to pull out a tangle.

Ben had made an effort. He'd baked sweet-potato crisps. He'd found the embroidered white tablecloth she'd bought at a car-boot sale and spread it on the slab table outside, just above the larger of the former tannery pits between the house and studio. It was where they liked to sit of an evening, there on the upper edge of town, watching shadows creep along the folds of ancient terraces on the fields opposite.

'Here's tae us; wha's like us? Damn few, and they're a'deid.' Maryann's late father's favourite toast. She did her best not to mangle the Scots as she raised her glass.

Ben didn't go straight into the subject, restraining himself, listening to her talk of the archivists' meeting that morning. Probate inventories had arrived. 'Katie's said they're our priority.' When she was finished, Ben leant forward. 'Now listen, you.'

She grinned and shook her head. 'I know what you're going to say. Before you start, I've rung the medical school.'

'The medical school? Where?' The conversation wasn't going the way he'd planned.

'Leeds.'

'We've only just got back here to live!' His hands tightened round the stem of his glass.

Maryann looked bewildered.

'To Settle.'

'Six years ago,' she reminded him, reaching across and topping up their wine. 'What's that got to do with it? Anyway, I've rung the medical school and they're going to-'

'No!' He threw up his hands, the afternoon's calm lost. Glass and wine spread across the tablecloth. The blackbird on top of the shed roof stopped his hectoring song. Ben stared at it, then back at Maryann, sitting there unconcerned. The slanting sun lit up her rust-red hair as if a halo, he thought. 'Maryann,' he took a deep breath. 'We discussed this. We'd be buried. That way we can go and talk to each other at the graveside, commune with each other.'

'Did I agree?' She frowned. 'When did I agree? I don't think I did.'

'Oh, for God's sake!' Ben pushed back his chair, forgetting it was on grass, and nearly tripped on it in his hurry to get up.

Maryann watched him lope into the house. They were in their early fifties and still his walk was coltish as if at any moment he'd break into a run. Blue jumper and trousers went into the gloom of the house.

She hadn't expected this. She'd been so sure, with his being the more socially responsible of the two of them, that he'd approve of her plan. She'd forgotten the earlier conversation, more than a year before, about visiting each other's graves. She picked up the shards of glass thoughtfully. A drop of blood landed in the spread of wine, and another.

Hands on her shoulders. He'd come out and she hadn't noticed, so intent had she been on her blood merging with the wine. 'My darling,' his voice shook. 'Are you sure you're not saying that you're ill?'

She reached up and covered his hand with hers. 'Quite sure. I'm just thinking ahead, being practical. I read an article about it. They *need* bodies, you see; not enough are avail-'

'I don't want this.' His fingers tightened. 'The idea of knives and saws going into you. It's appalling.'

'Then don't go there.' She swivelled round and smiled

up at him, at his blue eyes, sharp, as if they would impale her in his distress. She'd smudged blood on his hand from her cut. She licked it away.

He pulled back. 'I shan't be able to come to your grave and talk to you!'

'There is that,' she agreed. 'But you could talk to me in the air.' She waved an arm vaguely.

'But why now? We're still young.'

'-ish.' She composed her face; he wasn't smiling. 'Why not now? It's like having a donor card; even some twenty-year-olds carry those.'

'You haven't got a donor card.'

'I know I haven't. Nor have you. But we could have. Anyway, what's the difference?'

'Stop it! Stop being so bloody pragmatic. We're talking about death.' He sat down.

She shifted the broken glass away from him. 'Does it bother you so much, my love?'

'It does.'

'Oh.'

They sat in silence, he staring ahead, she sucking her cut. It had stopped bleeding. She was the first to reach out again. 'I'm sorry,' she said, and with that, Ben felt both reassured and relieved.

Three

Next day Ben's painting began to go better: the colours seemed less circus-like, less fanciful, more as if they were delving into the earth's depths; and the figures to the top right of the picture at last achieved the dynamic that he'd been searching for which had, till now, proved elusive.

He painted on, waiting for Maryann to come and call him, to say she was home from work. He was lost in purples and greens, unaware that sunshine was leaving the garden. He painted on till he was satisfied, then cleaned his brushes and threw away the dirty water, hung his overall on the back of the door, and went out, slotting back the latch. Outside, the sky was streaking red and purple and he realized his hunger. In the house, he went whistling upstairs, splashed his face, scrubbed his hands. Down below again, he poured himself a beer and rang Maryann.

'Hi, it's Maryann Waugh. Sorry I can't talk just now, but leave a message and I'll return your call. Later today,

I hope.'

'Will you be back soon? I'm hungry!' He texted too, for good measure. 'Back soon? Come home. Love you.'

He put water on to boil for pasta. From the marshy patch outside he tore watercress. He took dried tomatoes from their jar of oil, crushed garlic, and chopped all together. In the fridge was feta.

'I'm sorry, love.' She rushed in, cheeks flushed. 'I've had such a day! A stash of papers and ledgers to do with building the Ribblehead railway viaduct has come to light and Katie asked if I'd go up to fetch it. There was a man I got talking to on the train up. He said he'd retired from farming, and I said I didn't think farmers retired, and he said well, this one did; his son and daughter-in-law have taken over and he and his wife are in a bungalow in town which is warm and cosy and has a small garden. Anyway, he asked me if I'm careful to look after the wildlife, especially in winter. Birds and stuff. He said they've a couple of hedgehogs that appear from time to time, so they don't use slug pellets. Instead, his wife puts out a saucer of beer for the slugs to come to and drown themselves in. When she's out, he rescues the slugs from the saucer, takes them to the shed at the bottom of the garden and feeds them water and then releases them, back into the garden!

'Anyway. On the way back, I skimmed through the papers. Listen to this,' and she took a scrap of paper from her pocket. '"A horde of navvies, alien in character and behaviour, invaded the somnolent town of Settle." I bet that caused a-'

'Whoa! Take a breath!'

She stopped, laughed. 'I'll tell you more over dinner.'

'Come to the studio first.'

'Now? You've finished the painting?' In his studio, she looked long at the picture. 'It's good. The way the cotton grass sways.' She squeezed his arm. 'Makes me think of that time we stopped on the tops and fell asleep, remember? There's joy in it. Brooding, too.'

He cocked his head, unsure about the brooding.

'At this rate, you'll be ready for your exhibition, no problem.'

Back in the kitchen, she took over the cooking: 'I need to be doing, I'm speeding too much to sit still. Oh, before I forget, Katie's asked if we'd like to go over for Sunday lunch.'

'Mm.' He stuffed crisps in his mouth. 'If this weather holds, we could leave the car and cycle over; it'd take only a bit over an hour.'

'Good idea. Those nineteenth-century navvies – can you imagine the disruption in town?'

The phone rang. 'Hang on.' Ben reached for it. 'Hello, Son.' It was their standard greeting: hello, Dad, hello, Son. 'What news?'

'Are you now... Guatemala! ... with...?'

At the cooker, Maryann, trying to make out the conversation, put down the spoon. 'Can I speak to him?' she mouthed.

'Your mother wants a word. Oh, all right.' He shook his head at her. 'Goodbye then, have fun.'

'He was in a hurry.'

'I gathered that.'

'He was at the airport. He said he'll be up to see us soon. Sends you his love. They're going off to Guatemala, on a hiking holiday.'

'They?'

'A woman.'

'Ah.'

'Exactly, ah.'

'You never know.' They grinned at each other.

'Maybe she'll stop him banking.'

'She might be a banker herself.'

'Oh, please. One's quite enough. Anyway, we're going way too fast, Ben.'

'At least she's adventurous. Now, tell me.'

Maryann put the bowl of pasta on the table. 'Well.

There was a reference, rather slighting, to the local women caught up in the excitement, who went to the viaduct settlements with the navvies. And there are housing inspectors' reports from the 1870s. That's all I was able to glean in the time between Ribblehead and Settle stations. I'm itching to get to work on it and see what else is there.'

Four

Inside the archive office, grey desks were unoccupied, the hum of computers stilled, papers and books cleared away. Except in the corner by the window. There one sharp light shone from a screen, ignored by Maryann, who was frowning down at a sheet of paper that had fallen out of the Ribblehead archive. A woman had walked out on her young family. Five children. Or six; the number had been crossed out to make it five. No further detail was given.

Maryann stretched and rolled her head and only then noticed the time. She shut down the computer and set off for home. Lights were coming on in the houses around the green by the time she crossed it. It was so peaceful, round by their back door. Through the window she could see Ben stretched out on the sofa, reading the paper, picking at nuts from a bowl at his side. The grass at her feet was already thick with dew, the smells moist and earthy. She imagined the different smells from when it had been a tannery, wrinkling up her nose at the thought of the stench and slop of manure. From a blackcurrant bush at her side she plucked a leaf and crushed it; its fruity smell drove out the idea of stench, and Ben was at the door. 'What time do you call this?' mockingly, hands on hips.

'I know.' They hugged. 'There's so much in those Ribblehead papers, it was difficult to get away.'

'What's the rustling?'

Maryann pulled away and felt in her pocket. 'Oh. I didn't know I'd put it in there. I must remember to take it back.' She folded the paper and returned it to her pocket. 'It's a reference to a woman from up at Dent Head, the highest settlement for the railway workers. She walked out on her young family. But – oh, I don't know – why the reference? It feels out of place.'

Next day Maryann slipped the paper back in the file, and gave priority to one of the probate inventories.

But the paper nagged at her. It nagged at her all morning, through the archivists' lunch meeting and into the dark, rainy afternoon. The woman might have been one of the camp followers from Settle. The navvies would have had to stay in town at first, waiting for their cabins to be built. The railway's engineers, those better off, could have stayed in the local inns. On a whim, she fetched the archive's photocopied census returns from the time and pushed away her keyboard to give more space. Her finger ran down the entries, looking at the professions' column. Lodgers were mentioned at three of the inns, the Royal Oak, the Talbot and the Spread Eagle.

She fetched leather-bound ledgers from the inns. The takings of each had swelled in the late 1860s. Her left hand reached up to turn on the desk light while her right scribbled down notes. In the Spread Eagle accounts, the hand that entered the accounts had added a paragraph at the end of each year and occasionally during it. An entry in late May read: 'Absconded north to the viaduct workings: an orphan lass to whom we gave lodging and charity. She came with a good character from the schoolmaster, whom she assisted at the school, and from his wife, too. We permitted her to serve in the evenings. Alas, she has betrayed our trust. An Irish railway engineer disgraced her in the woods.'

Maryann referred back to the census. The Spread Eagle Inn, Kirkgate, Landlord William Duckett, Wife Elizabeth – both born in Settle; one lodger, a railway engineer Erin O'Beirne, born in Cork. She smiled. House servant: Dinah Peters, born in Settle.

She leaned back, pressing her thumbs into the

corners of her eyes, tired from examining cramped copperplate entries. As she set off home, she tried to imagine the attraction of a silver-tongued Irish stranger, one with money, too, since the engineers were paid quite well. And the sweetness of bluebells in the woods in May, crushed under entangled bodies.

Ben met her halfway up the hill and they went on together. 'I really feel the need of a decent walk,' he said, 'don't you? I was thinking we could do that on Friday.'

She frowned. 'Well - there's a lot on. The probate inventories need sorting and then there's this Ribblehead material.'

'Can't that wait?'

She rubbed her nose. 'Maybe it can, but I'm not sure that I can. It's rich stuff.'

'You're supposed to be on a four-day contract. Come on, we could both do with some time off.'

Five

The days passed quickly enough till Friday when Maryann awoke, dull and uneasy, her mouth dry. The bed felt unfamiliar. She lay a while, quite still, trying to place herself. She shifted onto her side to snuggle up to Ben, but the sheets beside her were cool and empty.

Then there he was, with a tray.

'I woke up and you weren't here.' She stretched up for him. 'You're already dressed! Have you been up long?'

'Yes, sleepyhead. I've done a good hour in the studio. It's nine o'clock. We're off on a walk - remember? So tea, breakfast, and we can go? I got bacon from the butcher for a fry-up.' He pulled the curtains open, letting sun stream in.

She hoisted herself up on the pillows, and cleared her throat. 'Oh, right. I had a weird dream.'

Ben poured the tea, passed her a cup. 'Tell me.'

'I'm in a city, trying to go home. I stop, and people come up and ask me where I want to go. Suddenly I'm in another street and walking, and people still come up and ask me. And then the street isn't tarmac; it's the texture of a bog and I'm barefoot and sinking into cold mud. Everyone is helpful and kind. But the trouble is, I don't know where I want to go; I don't know the house, I don't even know the road.' She gazed blindly out of the window, her head still muzzy.

'Well, the road today is towards Feizor,' Ben said briskly. 'You would like to, wouldn't you?' His voice was so eager and his eyes bright, how could she not, and gradually the disorientation from the dream faded.

After breakfast they grabbed hunks of bread and crumbly Wensleydale cheese, apples and elderflower cordial and set off, across the town and over the river, towards the church where a path wound through the old part of the churchyard.

'I lay down in that,' Ben said as they passed an open sarcophagus. 'Harry dared me to. We must have been about nine.'

'You've never told me that before. Were you scared?'

'Terrified. But I did it and I lived to tell the tale.'

'I wish sheep still grazed here,' Maryann said wistfully, 'the way they did when we were children.'

'We could book a grave,' Ben said suddenly. 'We can, you know.'

'Whatever for?'

'Well, look: they're running out of space. In the past,' he said, his eyes caught by the skull and crossbones on one tombstone, 'people meditated on death. Trappist monks lay in their coffins at night to remind them of their mortality, and that they should live to God's glory every day, every moment. Philosophers kept a skull to hand.'

'In paintings, at any rate.'

'Now it's all stay alive at any cost and then recycle where possible and then cremate. All practical, no contemplation.'

'She wasn't buried, you know.'

'What?'

'That woman, the one I was telling you about. I can't find a record of any burial; there ought to be one.'

'Maryann? Shall we… book a grave?'

But she'd gone ahead on the path and didn't answer. It wound upwards through overgrown brambles, past houses to a track through the woods until at last they were climbing towards the old quarry and a flat bit of moor where wild raspberries grew. They picked and ate, walked on through fields of shorthorn cattle, brown coats glossy in the sunshine, and on to the farm tea shop to gorge on scones, before returning home the long way round, some of the time talking, mostly in companionable silence, calm and at peace.

Later, in bed, Maryann caught Ben's intent expression. 'What?' She hoisted herself on one elbow to look at him. 'What are you thinking about?'

'That day in France.'

'Mm?'

'The hot day, just before Harry and Justine's wedding. There was a field on a slope, a wood at the edge and a stream trickling clear, winding down through the grass.'

'There were dragonflies. Their wings caught the sun like tiny rainbows. Do you remember?'

'Don't interrupt!' He tapped her nose with his finger. 'I'm the one painting a picture here.'

She smiled sleepily at him. 'Sorry.'

'Dragonflies, over the water.'

'And I cupped my hands with water,' Maryann added anyway.

'And I drank.'

'No one was around.'

'And then we went over to the shade of a tree. With one thing on our minds. Come here, you.' Ben reached out for her.

Six

On Sunday it was cooler as they cycled to a late Sunday lunch. 'I doubt that we'll eat before three,' Katie had said. They climbed narrow lanes with the moors spread in greys and greens and mauves about them, and Pen-y-Ghent higher in the distance, down steeply across wooded becks, hemmed in by drystone walls, up the next hill till again the world lay before them, until, finally, over two cattle grids and along a stony track, they'd reached their friends' house, solitary, sunken into the stony moor.

'Can I help?' Maryann asked, leaning in the kitchen doorway, watching Katie. With her cropped hair and black clothes, Katie looked boyish and not in her late-fifties at all.

'Certainly not. Go through and have a drink with the others. Take Jackson with you!' she called after her.

'Come on, dog.' Jackson trotted out and stopped in the hall. He glanced at her then turned to the floor-length mirror, moving his black head to one side and then to the other, rough hair sticking up. He seemed to frown at his mirror dog then grin, tongue lolling out.

Maryann went and stood beside him. 'Practising expressions, are you?' She twisted her face into an approximation of a monster.

'There you are,' said Ben, coming out to find her. 'What a face! Oh, hello, Jackson,' as the dog bounded over. He bent to scratch its ears.

'Let's get a dog,' Maryann said impulsively, 'a Jack Russell like this one, all character.'

'Think about it. Jackson's great but he'd be a pain on long walks, with the sheep and cattle, and going after rabbits.'

'And getting entangled in our legs. I suppose you're right. If you died, though, and I was unfleet of foot, I think I'd get one then. I bet you would, too.'

'There you go again.'

'What?'

'Talking about death.'

'We're not. We're talking about dogs.'

'Have it your own way.'

'Hey, don't sulk.' She flicked his ear as they went on through. Inside, a stove burned, its flames leaping clear.

'Come and sit down. Is it your usual, a G and T?' Tim's eyebrows rose and fell comically. Maryann liked him, liked his face lined from heavy smoking in the past, liked his enthusiasm for jazz. 'I saw Becky at the auction,' he said, 'Wednesday evening. She sends her love.' He handed Maryann a glass. It'd be generous on the gin, Maryann warned herself.

'She was selling cows - limousins - got a pretty good price for them, too,' he went on.

'You should know, being auctioneer. Becky must find it hard sometimes, farming on her own, the way she likes to talk.'

'Don't you believe it, Ben!' Tim retorted. 'She chatters to the animals.'

'She does,' Maryann chimed in, 'you must have noticed. I wish we saw more of her,' she added. 'She isn't so very far away, but still.'

'And Justine and Harry, how are they?' asked Tim. 'How's Justine coping with the latest health-service shake-up?'

'Grumbling,' said Maryann, 'in a very French sort of way.'

'Furious,' said Ben.

'Ah.'

'We try not to bring up the subject of medicine when we see her.'

'Of course not. She needs the break.' Katie came in

to join them.

They stayed long at the table. 'Delicious, such a treat.' Maryann leaned back in her chair and stretched. 'We ought to set off.'

'Before it's dark.'

'Ben, it's virtually dark already.' Tim lit the candles, making the point. 'So you may as well stay a little longer. Have another coffee.'

'It'll do no harm to be a bit late for work tomorrow, not the way you've been going at it,' Katie added. 'She's working too hard.'

'Tell me about it,' Ben muttered. He pushed his cup forward.

Maryann smiled at them, conceding. 'Then yes, coffee would be lovely, thanks.'

Katie, pouring it, took a deep breath. 'Have you two ever done Ouija?'

They shook their heads.

'Tim and I were talking about it this morning. We haven't either, and we'd quite like to try. On the grounds of doing everything just once.'

'Oh go on. I'm all for new experiences.' Maryann's eyes shone.

'Have you got an Ouija board?' Ben was less keen.

'You don't need one.' Katie was already on her feet.

She returned with paper and scissors and pens. 'Here we go.'

Her enthusiasm and Maryann's was catching. They cleared the table of wine glasses and coffee cups and the debris of chocolate-gingers and nuts, laid out white squares of paper each with a letter of the alphabet in sequence, and placed a glass in the centre, upturned.

'There's a fog gathering out there,' said Tim coming in from the barn, his arms full of wood.

Maryann glanced out of the window. Fingers of mist were reaching out towards the glass, curling and beckoning. She shivered. 'Shall I draw the curtains?'

'Good idea. Let's make it really snug.'

'That settles it. Stay the night,' Tim urged. 'You'd be mad to cycle back now.'

Ben was relieved. He wanted to go home, but not in the damp chill of fog. It would have been just like Maryann to say that they'd cycle anyway but, curiously, she seemed content to stay.

'Ready?' asked Katie.

'Yes,' said Tim, turning off all lights and returning to the table. Now there was just red firelight and the three candles on the windowsill.

'Fingers on the glass - gently,' said Katie.

'Now what?' Maryann asked, when all their fingers

were resting on it.

'We wait. Till the glass moves. Concentrate.' She intoned, 'Spirit of the glass, we are here.'

Nothing happened. Maryann laughed.

'Ssh. Is anyone there? Spirit of the glass, we are waiting,' Katie called out, singsong.

The glass shuddered. It jerked. Ben's finger fell off it.

'Put it back,' Katie hissed.

Slowly, the glass set off across the table, away from Ben, till his arm was stretched out.

'F.' Tim called out the letter where it stopped.

It went sideways. 'I.'

And again. 'N.'

It stopped. 'FIN?' Maryann spelled out. 'What's FIN?' She laughed abruptly.

'Maybe the spirit is French and it's *fin*, the end, finish.' Ben took his finger away. 'Don't take it off,' said Katie.

As if on cue, the glass trembled and went back till it pointed to D.

It paused again. Then slid to W near Ben, back across to E, R and back to E, so fast that it was difficult for them to keep their fingers on it.

'FIND WERE. Makes no sense,' said Tim, frowning in concentration.

I followed quickly. Pause. It moved sideways.

L, back to I, on to E. FIND WERE I LIE.

'Find where I lie. The "were" was a spelling slip. Who are you, spirit of the glass?' asked Katie.

Maryann's hand crept into Ben's under the table. He glanced at her, but she was intent on the glass, eyes narrowed.

U.

P. Pause. Then fast, so fast it was difficult to keep pace. BY.

'Up by,' whispered Maryann.

R.

'No.' Ben took away his fingers, pushed back his chair. 'Enough. I don't like this. Maryann, is it you moving the glass?'

There was a dazed look in her eyes as she shook her head. 'I'm following it, like you. Like, all of us. I mean, we're all... aren't we? No one's steering it, are you? Katie?'

Katie looked uncertain. 'I'm not.'

'Nor am I. Creepy.' Tim looked round at them. 'Mind, if none of us is doing it, what is?'

'Our collective consciousness?'

A draught sent the candle flames leaping sideways; the four at the table were caught as if carved into gargoyles, eyes sunk in sockets, cheeks drained pale.

Tim shoved back his chair and turned on the light. Katie gathered up the letters. 'Scraps of paper,' she said, 'that's all they are, and a glass. We did it ourselves.' She took them through to the kitchen and there was the sound of a bin lid opening and closing. 'How about a nightcap, Tim?'

'Of course. What'll it be? We've a decent cognac, or there's homemade blackberry liqueur or amaretto?'

They didn't refer to the Ouija again, and went to bed, the creak and sigh of old timbers settling with them, blanketed by the mist around the house.

Seven

Both Ben and Maryann continued working late, Ben making sure he had enough work ready for his forthcoming exhibition, and Maryann taking advantage of that to work on her research at the end of each day.

Mid-week, though, they joined Harry, Ben's friend from childhood, and his wife Justine for a film. 'Fancy coming to the Hart's Head for a drink? We left the car up there. I'd been out with a patient and Harry came to meet me.' Justine pulled on her jacket, yanking out thick, wild hair from its collar.

'Because she thought it'd do me good to walk into town for the movie and back again,' Harry explained wryly, 'lose some of this.' He patted his belly.

When they were seated in the pub, Ben said, 'That woman's disappearance in the movie is a bit like your woman's, isn't it.'

'Your woman's? What's this?' Justine leaned forward, curious.

'Oh, something I've come across when researching.'

Maryann was dismissive.

'Go on, love,' Ben prompted her. 'The shanty towns at Ribblehead for the viaduct, and a woman vanishing from the record.'

'No, beyond Ribblehead, up at Dent Head north of Blea Moor. The workers' cabins there were the worst. One year, the summer of 1872, when it rained twice as much as usual, they would have been islands in a sea of claggy mud. The only way to survive in that bog was to drink.' She clammed up.

'Go on,' Ben said, 'tell us more, like what happened to that woman.'

'Actually,' Maryann said, backing off, 'I'd rather save it till I find out more.'

'Oh, shame. Are you feeling superstitious? You English!'

Ben laughed. 'Don't take it personally, Justine. She's only tossed me the bare bones,' he said, 'so far.'

'The bare bones of what?' asked Harry, lumbering back from the bar with their drinks, belly leading the way.

'*Cochon*,' said Justine, as he put a bowl of chunky chips on the table and dived in.

'You used to be such a skinny runt,' Ben said, mocking him.

'You, too.'

'I still am.'

'The bare bones of what?' Harry repeated, ignoring Ben.

'Maryann's research. She's got her teeth into it, like a terrier shaking a bone.'

'So tell us, Maryann.' Harry swigged his beer.

Maryann shook her head and once Ben got on to his current enthusiasm about natural not chemical pigments in paint, she felt able to zone out. Ben was right: the woman had got under her skin. Even Katie had passed comment, concerned that she was concentrating so much on the Ribblehead research that the probate inventories were languishing.

Suddenly she heard a cry, desolate and lonely, the cry of a curlew. She looked wide-eyed at the others. They were laughing at something Harry had said, but their laughter was silent to her. It was as if she was separated from them, separated from the hum of voices and clink of glass. Instead there was grass, and earth, in her nostrils. Puzzled, she closed her eyes. In the red haze behind her eyelids, she saw a woman dart from the shelter of one rock to another, crouching low, apparently so that men carrying a coffin didn't notice her. They rested it on a long flat stone. The men stretched their arms, flexed their muscles. They took out clay pipes and started tamping them. The woman leaned against the stone, and, tired, she closed her eyes.

She didn't see the man come round the back of her, she didn't turn in time.

Maryann did. Her eyes snapped open as she gasped.

'Are you all right?' Justine was leaning forward, her hand on Maryann's arm.

Maryann blinked. The scene had come and faded in a heartbeat. At the other side of the table, Ben and Harry were deep in conversation, 'funding,' she heard, 'cuts'. 'I must go to the loo.' She scrambled to her feet. 'I'll be right back.' In the ladies, she gagged, on nothing. She rested her face against the mirror, then splashed on cold water, and returned. 'Sorry about that. I'm fine. The film must have affected me.' She smiled.

Justine smiled back, a little uneasily, and drew her into the conversation.

It was dark when they left the pub. 'Can we give you a lift back?'

Ben and Maryann looked at each other, and shook their heads.

'OK. Sleep well, you,' Justine said to Maryann. 'You're looking tired.'

Maryann pulled a face. 'I have peculiar dreams;

they're unsettling. It'll pass.'

As they went down stone steps from the pub, Maryann halted.

Ben, looking back, saw her face in shadow from the clouds over the moon.

'It's weird. I keep seeing gaps and holes in steps and stairs through which I could fall.'

'Vertigo? Shall I buy you a zimmer frame?' he teased.

She frowned. 'It's not like that. It's more like *Alice in Wonderland* moments, you know?'

Ben pulled his ear. 'Not really, no. But I like that, you being Alice. You could be any name you wanted, and I'd like you.'

She smiled at his fondness. 'That's all right then.'

They passed only two people on the way home, the first in the ginnel heading down to the river. 'Good evening,' Ben greeted him, and Maryann, 'Hello.'

Nothing back.

'Have you noticed?' Maryann said as they walked on down between the high walls that hemmed them in on either side, before coming out above the river. 'Have you noticed that hardly any people greet you in the dark whereas all do in daylight?'

'Perfectly reasonable,' said Ben. 'They think you might be armed and dangerous.'

'Or a ghost.' She linked her arm through his and squeezed it.

Eight

'Look: a postcard from Adam.'

'Let's see?' She took it from him with fingers wet from washing up. 'Rio! I thought they were in Guatemala.'

'Good of him to let us know,' Ben grumbled.

'Oh, you.' She swiped him with the card then dropped it on the table. 'Be glad he sends us postcards. He says it's business. Pleasure, though, too.'

'I bet it is.'

'Grump.' She kissed his head. 'Envious?'

'Not at all.' He caught her eye and smiled. 'I'd rather be a painter than a banker, and I'm happy here. At least this awful job of his gets him to interesting places, and he is enjoying himself.'

She turned back to the sink.

'And a letter from Mother.' Ben's mother had married Maryann's father after years of warm friendship and they'd moved to Somerset to teach. Now a widow, she was wheelchair-bound and in special accommodation, drawing a pension and writing letters.

'I'll leave it to you to open this time.'

'No, you. Read it to me.'

Ben was slitting open the envelope when his eye caught a larger one. 'Maryann.'

'Mmm?'

'What's this? There's something here for you, from Leeds University, School of Medicine. Munchkin?'

She hesitated. 'Open it, if you want.'

He slit it open. 'There's a booklet: "Bequest Information – Information for those who wish to donate their body for anatomical examination, and instructions for next of kin or executor". He turned to the accompanying letter and read, first in silence, then aloud. '"Dear Ms Waugh, Thank you for your kind enquiry regarding the donation of your body . . ." Does "the next of kin or executor" not get a say?' His voice had gone quiet and precise. 'I thought we'd sorted this.'

She gazed round at him. 'Ben, listen. It's a good thing to-'

'But I can't bear it!'

She didn't speak.

'Does that mean you'd do this whatever I said?'

'I haven't decided yet. Would you honour my wishes if I did?'

'I would always honour your wishes. But why,

Maryann?' They stared at one another. 'Oh, I get it. Finally. This is because of your brother, isn't it.'

'Maybe.' She shrugged. 'I do feel I should give something back for all they did for him.'

'He died,' Ben said flatly.

She snorted. 'I know that. But the care they gave him, all those months of one-to-one nursing, the way they treated him, with respect, affection, even.'

'You don't carry a debt for him. What about me?' Ben was immediately ashamed and the words hung in the air between them. He felt like a spoilt brat. He was trying to stay calm, outwardly at least, though his heart sped like a woodpecker's drumming and a headache threatened.

'I haven't decided yet. And of course I care what you think, all right?'

She waited for Ben to respond. When he didn't, she turned back to the sink.

He stared down at the table, pressed his finger in circles over its top till the glass squeaked. He slid back his chair. 'Drink?' he asked.

'Please,' Maryann answered, just as briskly.

'Wine or elderflower?'

'Wine.'

When they got to bed, she lay on her back and

pondered, as his breathing settled into sighs and he fell asleep.

Nine

Flowerpot men were sprouting over town that week, a community initiative. New ones appeared wherever you looked. Most were outside. One lolled in a wheelbarrow, drunkenly singing - according to a paper stuck on its chest - 'Show me the way to go home', Ben and Maryann's favourite to sing on a long walk if wet and tired. Rooney and wife, complete with handbag, appeared on a garden wall, dejected, back from football failure. Biggles touched down in his machine - another wheelbarrow, but this one with wings - at the start of the steep hill to Kirkby Malham. Two small flowerpot women were seated in a hairdresser's window, pink rollers in their flowerpot hair. A flowerpot spider squatted huge and black on the wall of the shoemaker and a flowerpot postman took a break on the bench outside the post office. Outside the newsagent's, another read a paper bought from inside. And more and more, every day, until it felt as though a hitherto unknown group of inhabitants living below ground had at last decided to show themselves and bask in the daylight.

But Ben, cross with Maryann, refused to get interested. Anyway, he had to get on with his paintings. He worked fiercely on a figure crossing a bog; only when you looked closely could you make out that it, too, had a flowerpot head and small jointed flowerpot arms, an intrusion of cultivation into primitive nature.

'I've asked a church warden about booking a grave; we can do that, you know.'

Maryann stared at Ben.

'They have to put up a notice, or perhaps two, I'll have to ask again; it's rather like getting planning permission,' Ben rushed on. 'Here.' He pushed a cup of coffee across the breakfast table to her.

'We don't need to book a grave,' she said flatly after a silence. 'There's plenty of room in the churchyard. Anyway, why? We're both fit and well.'

'So why might you be willing your body to the medical school?' Ben sounded triumphant.

'Oh, leave it, Ben.' She pushed away the cup, hoisted her bag on her shoulder, declared 'I'm off,' bestowed a peremptory kiss somewhere near his lips and was out of the door, heading for work.

Later, returning from swimming in the river, Ben found Maryann at the round dining table, all dark polished wood, that stood in front of the great fireplace. They only used the dining room for special occasions, for making an effort with their cooking for friends or at Christmas and Easter, for spreading out bank stuff and trying to make sense of it, and for solemn family conferences. But she was sitting, quite still, with no papers in front of her.

'I'll make us tea,' he said, after watching her.

She stirred. 'Thanks. There's no cake.'

'No matter. On the bench?'

'Remember how some of my information's come from loose pages?' she said, taking the mug of thick tea from him. 'I wondered if they might come from a journal. And now a journal has come to light, and I think it's the one, judging from style and handwriting. It was by a missionary, called William Fletcher, who worked up the railway line in the 1870s. It's a real bit of luck. Listen to this,' and she took a paper from her pocket and read out:

December 31
It has been a very severe frost for a week past and with the occasional falls of snow it has made

bad travelling. Six huts have been erected at Dent Head. In the second is an Irish man who won't hear anything I have got to say. 'And you,' I asked, turning to the woman. 'Let me lead you to Christ.' I instructed her to own her sin and her need of salvation. But after praying for the Holy Spirit to enlighten her dark mind I left with very bad feelings respecting her. I left her the tract 'How to come to Jesus'.

'I think she could be my woman.' She was calmly triumphant. 'I've written this. Listen:

'Dinah, possibly an orphan, found work helping the schoolmaster. Also a second job as a barmaid at the Spread Eagle, for which they let her stay in a box room. Then one night, on St Patrick's Eve, she met Erin, a young engineer, with his one grey eye, one green, and his smart, thin smile. He returned cruel English wit with Irish banter, and when he was with his own people he relaxed. Before two months were out, they'd lain among bluebells up in Cleatop Wood, overwhelmed by the sweet, moist scent.

He'd made good money laying railroads in America and had heard that good money was to be made here, too. She should go with him to the railway workings, he said, and he'd find a priest to marry them. By then she was sick in the mornings and needed little persuasion, and so she'd gone with him, to the black boggy land high above Dent village, where at first they shared a cabin with another couple. The moors frightened her and she was reserved with the neighbours. When fever visited the settlement, it caught both Dinah and Erin. They survived, but Dinah lost the baby she was carrying.'

Ben broke the silence. 'You found that out from the journal?'

'Not exactly. From the census and other records, and from joining up the dots.'

'Right,' he said drily.

'And I seem to see it.'

'You see it,' Ben repeated. 'Really?'

'It's as if the woman's wanting me to give her voice.' Maryann sighed at his expression. 'You think I'm being fanciful.'

'I didn't say that.'

'You didn't need to. You think I don't realize how odd it sounds?' She looked embarrassed. 'I wish I hadn't told you now.'

Ten

Two mornings later, Maryann was at the window, her back to him, quite still. The sun caught silver in her red curls.

He got up and put his arm around her, the warmth of his hip flowing into her through her light kimono. 'What's up, love?'

She sighed, leaned her head back against him. 'Us. Being irritated with each other. I hate it.'

'So do I.' His hand tightened. They stood in silence looking out. The fields with their strong walls, stone piled on stone, at the stream which rose from the centre of the sloping field and gathered pace till it went underground at the allotments, at the trees beyond the rising hill. The sky was pastorally blue, sheep dotted the green with white, and swallows flitted and swooped. There was no cause for misery, how could there be? Ben smiled. 'I love you.'

'I know.'

'Remember the evening we met again, at the Plough?

Funny that: a pub in Bloomsbury being named after a farm machine.'

It had been a hot day in London. One of those days when the air hangs heavy over the city, and the grass of the squares and parks is dry and dusty. One of those days which has you longing for the relief of rain. One of those days that reminds you that you want to be in France or back north, to swim in a river, to laugh in the sun, clean and clear, not muggy as in the city, swirling with traffic fumes. Ben had walked into the Plough and seen her, perched at the bar, one of a group, from work, he assumed: it was six-ish.

He'd ordered. 'Half a bitter, please,' and taken it round the side to see the woman whose swinging foot seemed to beckon.

From his side, he watched, felt a jolt of familiarity but couldn't quite place it till she spoke. He heard Yorkshire in her vowels. She laughed and her gurgling, joyous laughter touched a nerve, and he'd remembered.

She'd looked up then and seen him. He raised his glass to her.

She stopped in mid-conversation. 'Excuse me,' he heard her say as she slipped off the stool and came over and stood in front of him, frowning. Then her face cleared and a smile slowly spread. 'Ben! Ben – it is you, isn't it? Tell me I'm not daft.' She touched his arm and they were laughing.

'Friends of yours?' he asked, nodding at the group.

She nodded. 'Colleagues, friends. Not as much as you though. It's been years. Let's go.'

And that had led to where they were now.

Maryann sighed again, pressing deeper into his side. 'Do you need to paint this morning? You're almost ready for the exhibition, aren't you? We could take the day off. We could take the train up to Ribblehead and walk.'

'Why not?' He spun her round, hugged her tightly to him, her head against his chest. When she emerged for air, she clapped, her mood swiftly switched.

Leaving the station at Ribblehead, they walked down the track towards the viaduct, standing mighty over the landscape, man-made yet, like a cathedral, built to last in the wild land, austere, comforting, splendid. As they passed under the great arches, the sun warm on their backs, Maryann took off her jumper and tied it round her waist, and by the time they reached a farm gate, Ben followed suit.

'It'd be fun to rent this for a short holiday,' Maryann said, halting at the barn conversion. 'All those walks right on the doorstep.'

'Too pricey,' he said, walking on. 'Come on, you. We can always get the train for the walks.'

'We'd share costs with friends, it wouldn't just be us. I bet Harry and Justine would be interested; maybe Tim and Katie too. And Becky might come over. Oh-oh, you're really not keen.'

He grinned ruefully.

They passed through the second gate and turned to walk alongside the stream, shoes whispering in the long grass. Through another gate and to a wall where they began to veer off to the right.

Maryann stopped. She was shivering. 'Someone just walked over-'

'Don't say it! Hush! We're out for a walk.'

She was looking around, frowning. 'Breath on my face.'

Ben reached out and smoothed down her hair, which had blown about her face, even though he had felt no wind, not even a breeze.

'Let's go the other way.'

'I thought you wanted to head towards Dent.'

'I've changed my mind. Please.'

He shrugged. 'Fine. We could always get a bus back if we end up in Ingleton.'

They walked on in silence. 'You can't trust them,'

Maryann said suddenly, as they crossed a shallow ford.

'Trust what?'

'The moors.'

Ben was surprised. 'But you like the moors.'

'I do.' She shook her head briskly. 'It's just - a feeling. Oh, I'm probably being silly. Here.' She produced an apple from her pocket. 'You have first bite.'

Eleven

Maryann jolted awake. 'Ben!'

He was already out of bed and hauling on a dressing gown.

'Shall I come with you?'

He flapped a hand at her to stay, turned on their light, then the landing light. As he went on downstairs, turning on more lights as he came to them, he was as noisy as he could be to chase away the intruder, not wishing for confrontation.

It had been a dreadful sound. Like some large metal container, with stones in it, being dropped from a height onto stone floor and reverberating. Ben tried the front door. Locked, as it always was. Unless they were having people round, they didn't use it. He tried the back door. Locked. They didn't always bother locking that, but last night he had happened to. All windows were closed, apart from their bedroom window, wide open as usual, come calm or stormy weather. There was no intruder. Nothing was disturbed. Picking up a torch, he unlocked the kitchen door and went out. No wind. Clear night. He walked round the house. There was nothing and no one.

It was a puzzle. Back in the kitchen, he took pans from their hooks and dropped them onto the stone flags, trying to simulate the noise. They sounded tinny in comparison. He stretched into the low corner cupboard for the heavy cast-iron pan that he used for marmalade, lifted that and dropped it.

Maryann was in the doorway, shaking her head. 'Ben love, stop.'

'What could it have been?'

'I've no idea. Come back to bed.' He took the hand that she held out to him. And fell asleep at once.

'You know that landscape on the landing?'

Ben nodded, mouth full of yellow yolk and toast, eyes tired.

'I found it flat on the floor.'

'Fallen,' he muttered, after swallowing.

'Yes, but the cord wasn't broken and the hook in the wall was in place, not even bent. I hung it back. Didn't you notice that last night?'

He shook his head. 'Maybe I brushed against it and knocked it off on my way downstairs.'

Maryann wasn't convinced.

'Or you did, when you got up later,' he went on. 'Where did you go?'

'I had a rotten night. I kept imagining things - sounds, like explosions, in my head.'

'I'm not surprised, after that racket.'

'And there was a desolate moor. I got up and made myself chamomile tea. I thought it'd help if I moved.'

Curiously, they forgot the incident in the days that followed and life continued as normal. Until the evening that Ben came from his studio to the kitchen and found Maryann already there and starting to cook. 'I know it's your turn, but I got some haddock at the market. I didn't think you'd mind. Oh, and before I forget, I saw Justine in town. She said to tell you that Harry'll pick you up at ten tomorrow with his van - if that suits. But I expect he's texted you anyway.'

'He has.' He poured himself a beer and sat at the table watching her move round the room. Idly, he picked up an envelope that the postman had left on the table and opened it, not looking to see whether it was for him or for Maryann.

'Would you lay the table?' Maryann asked from the cooker.

Dear Ms Waugh,' he was reading.

He read on in disbelief. She'd actually rung them the morning after the booklet had arrived. 'We are most grateful to you for being prepared to help us in this generous and practical manner. Before signing the consent form, you asked about…'

'Maryann? Why are you doing this?'

'Mm?' She turned. 'Oh. I hadn't opened that yet. Is it from the medical school?'

'It is. You said you weren't going to do this.'

'Uh-huh.' She shook her head, rubbed absentmindedly at her cheek.

'You did. I distinctly heard you apologize.'

'Did I? I don't think I did. I'm sorry that you're taking it so hard. But I have to do it. Surely you can see that. It's so *right*, Ben. Why does it bother you so?'

'I've told you why.'

'Because of going to the graveside? Yes. But the rightness of this surely trumps that.'

He scrunched up the letter in fury and threw it on the floor, surprising himself at the welling up of emotion. 'You're so *obstinate*!'

'Takes one to know one,' she retorted, bending down to pick it up and smooth it out.

'Even cremation would be better. At least I'd have your ashes.'

'You'd only leave them on a shelf.'

'I wouldn't.' He stared at her, shocked. 'It's as if I don't know you.'

'Perhaps you don't.' Maryann regretted the words as soon as they were out. 'Let's leave it. There's no hurry.'

They ate almost in silence. She was calm, implacable, and Ben didn't know how to get through to her. He didn't even tell her how pleased he was that his paintings were ready for the exhibition. Not that she asked. After dinner he couldn't concentrate on his book and went up to bed, and when she came up too and got in, he rolled away from her.

Twelve

When Maryann got back home the next day, there was no Ben, but the voicemail light was blinking. 'Hello, it's me. Listen, there's been a problem. I tried your mobile but you must have it off. Anyway, Harry's had to leave his van at the garage. We can pick it up in the morning. The curator has suggested we go out to dinner and stay the night with him in Saltaire. It'd be good to get to know him better, and I'm all for it. OK? See you tomorrow.'

She'd left him that morning with Harry, loading his paintings into the van. They were still annoyed with each other. She'd turned back and hugged him fiercely, and was glad of that now. Truth be told, it was a relief to have him gone. She rubbed irritably at the makings of a cold sore on her lip as she pulled a file out of her bag and settled down to look at the notes she'd copied out. There were several entries from the preacher's journal.

September 13

One of the miners was killed at the bottom of No.1 shaft yesterday by the fall of a stone. He has left a widow and four small children unprovided for.

March 9

Another of the men has died of fever. He was an Irishman and has left six children.

She sucked a strand of hair. Neither felt as if they were about 'her' woman.

June 18

Caught in one of the most terrific thunderstorms I ever knew. Being on high ground the lightning blazed around me, the rain and hail came down in torrents and I was a mile and a half from any shelter. I was deeply impressed by the grandeur of the storm but had little fear and repeated the well known 'The God who rules on high thunders when it pleases him.'

June 19

Yesterday during the storm five miners were

trapped in the tunnel and the water filled it up to the heading. Four of the five were drowned. One survived. He was found standing with only his nose and the top of his head above water. They rescued him, more dead than alive, on a raft.

Then Maryann seemed to see, as clearly as the wood of the table under her arms, children huddled in the corner of a hut, eyes as wide as young birds' beaks, fixed on the men standing around their father who they'd lain on the mattress. 'Here, Missus,' she heard, 'he's the only one who lives.' The woman Dinah got on her knees and looked at him. She wrapped his pale, cold body round to get him warm, fed him hot herbs and sloppy porridge.

Maryann blinked and shook herself free of the vision, and looked back at the journal.

June 29

To Dent Head. Huts in a wretched condition even though the men are earning enough. It would help if they were whitewashed. A lack of everything except food and drink. I spoke to the survivor of the tunnel flood. I find men are generally very indifferent about religion unless they are on a Sick Bed or in grave crisis, then they appear very grateful for the attention bestowed upon them. The man, Erin, was Irish. 'It is a sign that you were saved from drowning,' I told him. 'Let me now lead you to Christ who will save you for ever.' He would not hear anything I had to say.

Again Maryann found herself dreaming, not dreaming, she didn't know, except that she was there, seeing through other eyes:

Erin cursed the preacher when he was gone, and cried out his disappointment at having to take the only job they'd give him once they heard his accent: blasting tunnels deep under the earth in half-darkness where candlelight didn't reach and you thought the walls would fall on you, where the air was foul. He cried out his bitterness at the easy way they mocked him, how in his heart, behind his smiles, he hated this God-forsaken place and longed for colour, for richness, God-damnit even for Latin and a priest's chanting. How he clung to Dinah that night!

But the next night, he went out and stayed out while she fell asleep in the chair, waiting for him. When he stumbled back, his breath was foul and sour from liquor, his knuckles raw from fighting, his skin icy cold.

It was after then that he became a regular, hardened drinker - and Dinah learned somehow to manage and survive. She began building a tiny garden on a high patch of ground, rocky but sheltered. She walked sometimes as far as the shed that served as a chapel and her walks to that point made her bolder. Gradually it turned the moors from bleak and hostile to places of joy and peace, each new moor unfolding itself from behind another, like waves on the sea. She gathered chamomile, feverfew and thyme from the moors. She pulled out valerian from stone walls where it fanned out in white and pink and purple, and replanted it among her stones. She picked raspberry leaves from the wild raspberry stalks on the slopes out of Dent, comfrey and wild garlic from the sides of paths, often taking the toddling children with her, for she had four now, twins one year and a boy and then a girl the next, whom she wanted to keep fit and well. She planted rhubarb and potatoes from cottage gardens near the village, sometimes asking, sometimes taking. People came to her for help with their ailments. She kept their cabin clean and read her two books over and over again till the words from *Wuthering Heights* and *Jane Eyre* were engraved on her mind, and she read to the children from *A Child's Garden of Verses*, all precious books that the Settle schoolmaster and his wife had given her.

And she was pregnant again.

Maryann shot to her feet, slamming shut the journal, and set off up the hill in the dark, feet pounding the lane, trying to obliterate the voices in her head, the words, the images. Calmer, back home, she made herself a hot drink and went to bed.

She awoke. The duvet had slipped down a little, and she turned onto her side to face the window, pulling it up as she went. In half-turn she froze. Behind her, a woman was weeping.

She gripped the duvet, stuck there in half-turn, shoulders tensed, nerves quivering, and listened to the sobbing, her mind on high alert. So long as she stayed still, the woman might not know she was there, would not hear, might not see her. The curtains at the open window hung limp in the summer's night. She listened for other sounds. No wind, no rain. No loud noise in the house, only that weeping. Her scalp crawled. She could see the edge of the tree outside where the curtains didn't meet; the night is never completely dark. The leaves on the trees were still.

Weeping.

'I wish God might strike me dead if I return to him again.' The soft voice came clearly through the tears.

Maryann was at home, on her own. She made herself remember not the previous haunting but her actions that evening, trying to shut out the closer sounds. She had locked the kitchen door. And bolted it. There could not be anyone else in the house with her.

The weeping went on. She lay rigid. She lost all sense of time until the dark broke up and patterns began to show in the curtains. Outside one bird sang. The room was silent now. Slowly she relaxed. Slowly she turned to face the bedroom door, the closed door. No one was there. Shapes took on shades of colour.

She got up, wincing at the stiffness in her shoulder from clutching the duvet. Outside on the landing, the painting was in its place. She checked the front door, back door; both were locked. She glanced in every room. She tugged on clothes and made coffee, put on an old jacket of Ben's and sat outside, staring out over the field and moor as the world awakened.

When Ben came back with Harry at the end of the day, pleased with progress at Salts Mill, and she told them about the weeping, they said she'd surely been asleep and dreamed it. She'd been in a fugue state, when you lose a sense of your own identity, said Harry; Justine had been telling him about the condition. Ben snorted, interrupting him before he could get into full flight. 'You've been working too hard,' he said. She knew they were both wrong, but Ben was too full of plans for the hanging of the paintings for her to say more.

'What's that on your lip?' Ben asked, when Harry had gone and he was clearing their mugs from the table.

'A cold sore again.'

'No kissing then.'

'Yup. No kissing. Sorry. It's so itchy! It looks awful, doesn't it.'

'It's not so bad. It just seems worse to you because you can feel it as well as see it.'

'So you really do see it.'

'Well, only just. I mean, I see your whole face.'

'And my cushion tummy.'

'That's only because recently we've been eating a bit more.'

'To fill the silences.'

He stared at her, saw tears welling up. 'I love you.'

'I know you do.' But she was turning away from him.

That night Ben woke up to find Maryann gone.

When, minutes later, she still wasn't back, he threw back the bedclothes, groped for his dressing gown and went out on the landing. Below, at the bottom of the stairs, light flickered dimly. He followed it, down to the dining-room table. Still no Maryann, but she had been there; he saw papers and her reading glasses. He went on through: no Maryann on the sofa or in the armchair which she liked to sit in sideways, her back against one arm, legs over the other. 'Maryann?' he called.

There was no answer.

Something made him look up at the window. A shape outside filled the frame.

A stab of fear gave way to relief as he realised that it was her, bulkier looking from the hands shoved into the pockets of a jacket.

'Munchkin,' he said, going the few steps to her outside the kitchen door, 'what's up?'

She looked at him wildly, eyes large. 'I had such a dream.'

'I was worried; I couldn't find you.'

She gazed back at the moor. 'I was out there, walking slowly, the way you do in a nightmare, only it was wilder, and there were explosions, like blasting.'

'You're getting way too bound up in that research of yours. Come on, love, back to bed.' He yawned. 'Tell me about it in the morning.'

She let him lead her back. 'Will you sing to me?' He was right; she was obsessed.

'Come close. Shut your eyes.' And he sang:

'When I was a bachelor, I lived all alone,
and worked at the weaver's trade,
And the only only thing that I did that was wrong,
was to woo a fair young maid.
I wooed her in the winter time
and in the summer too,
And the only only thing I did that was wrong
was to keep her from the foggy foggy dew.

One night she came to my bedside
as I lay fast asleep.
She laid her head upon my breast and
she began to weep.
She cried, she sighed, she damn near died,
she said, what shall I do?
So I hauled her into bed and I covered
up her head... '

'Are you asleep?' he whispered. When she didn't answer, he wrapped himself around her.

Thirteen

Maryann came back earlier from work the next afternoon. Ben poured them wine, but he felt unable to get through to her. 'Fancy a game of chess?'

'All right.'

'You don't have to.'

'No, really, it's fine.'

'I'm sorry,' she said, resigning, laying her king on its side. 'That wasn't much of a match, was it. I've been solidly in front of the computer. It's made me stale.'

'That and your lip. You're no fun.'

'Oh, don't.' She looked tearful.

'Hey, come on. I was only teasing. Do you want to tell me more about your nightmare last night?'

She hesitated then shook her head. 'I'd rather forget it. Listen, Becky rang this morning, after you'd gone to the studio.'

'Oh? How is she?'

'She's fine. She asked if I wanted to go over for the weekend; it's all a bit last-minute, but we've nothing on, have we. Justine is going. A girlie weekend, just the three of us. I think I'll go, if that's OK.'

'Of course it is.' He frowned at her. 'Come on, Munchkin. I hate this distance between us. '

She nodded mutely, reached out and touched his hand. 'So do I. Maybe it'd do us good to have a break from each other, just three days. Oh, don't look alarmed.'

'We're all right, aren't we?'

'Of course we are,' she reassured him.

'When you come back, let's talk, properly, about this body business.'

'All right. Look, I've got to get on, if I'm to clear my desk by the last train.'

'You're going tonight, already?'

'Yes.' They hugged, but each could feel the tension in the other. 'I'll be back.'

Fourteen

Ben dived for the phone. 'Becky? Hello.'

'Hello. Where have you been? I've been ringing and ringing.'

'Have you? I was in my studio.'

'Why don't you use your mobile?'

He didn't bother answering that. She knew his antediluvian views on mobile phones.

'Thank goodness you're there now.'

'I am. Maryann isn't back yet. Shall I get her to ring you when she turns up?'

He heard an intake of breath. 'That's just it, Ben. She won't be turning up.'

'What?' He straightened, concentrated on the phone. 'I don't understand.'

'She'd been swimming, said she wanted one last swim, down at the river, by the rock shelf. When she came back, she seemed a bit tired, a bit low. You know what that moor's like, coming up from the river, it's steep and you have to scramble? Well, I was in the kitchen cooking. We've been taking it in turn to cook. Maryann had asked for chicken, and it was my turn, so I'd killed one of my chickens and plucked it - neither of the others fancied doing that.' She laughed, a bit oddly. Where on earth was her gabbling leading to?

'So, anyway, I had my head in the cupboard seeing if there was any coconut milk in there, and Maryann was fetching us both a glass of wine.'

'Becky, slow down. What's this about?'

'Oh, Ben. I heard her fall.'

'I don't understand. What are you telling me?'

'Ben, she's collapsed. She's unconscious. Justine rang right away for an ambulance. They're taking her to Bradford. Justine is with her, because of her being a doctor.'

'Right.' He was instantly alert, wanted to waste no more time talking. 'I'll get the car and come. Now.'

'Ben, the car's here,' Becky reminded him.

'I'll cycle to Giggleswick station.' He glanced up at the kitchen clock, primed for action. 'There's a train in twenty minutes. I'll make it if I cycle fast.'

'I'll meet you. Ring me when you know what time you arrive.' Her voice faded as he pressed the off button. Wallet, he thought. Set of car keys. He unearthed his mobile phone from under a tea cosy in the kitchen drawer. Jacket, should it turn cold. Bicycle lock and keys.

He closed the door, fetched his bicycle from the shed, stuffed the jacket in the pannier, and cycled down the hill, round the bend, across the road, down, past the industrial estate, past bungalows, mini roundabout, up, along, waited for a gap in traffic on the main road, crossed it, cycled up the path, ducking to avoid overhanging branches, locked the bicycle in the shelter, jacket out, running as the train was pulling in.

'You're all right. I saw you,' the conductor greeted him as he stepped into the train, heart pounding, throat dry.

'Bradford, please.' He proffered money and subsided into a seat. Maryann in hospital, Maryann in intensive care, there'd be tubes and bleeping monitors.

His phone rang. It was Becky. 'Are you OK, Ben?'

'I'm in the train,' he said drily, and cut her off. He wanted to concentrate, not talk.

She was at the station waiting for him as he came out. 'I rang the hospital to tell them we, you, were on our way. But they've taken her to Leeds, not Bradford. She's had a CT scan already; she's in a coma. We're going to the Infirmary.'

They swung out onto the road. 'Ben? Ben? Did you hear? I'm taking us to Leeds.'

He had his eyes shut tight. Leeds Infirmary had to be good. She'd had an eye operation there when only two, and had luminous eyes to show for it, her loving eyes. 'God,' he prayed, 'dear God. Be with my Maryann. Keep her safe. Let her know I love her. Tell her I'm on my way. Be with her, tell her I love her, I always have, I always shall, God, God, God.'

'We'd been having such a good time. Maryann was OK. Well, she complained of a headache, but we'd had wine the night before, she wasn't the only one, you know how it is, and she took a paracetamol.'

Ben zoned in and out of her babbling stream of words, 'mm,' he said, 'mm,' and stared out as she drove, his mind calling to Maryann. 'I'm coming, Munchkin, I'm coming. Wait for me, I'm coming.'

Maryann died. Two days later. He hadn't left her bedside.

He sat there numbly. He sat through the nurse's touch on his shoulder, he took the cup of tea they put into his hand.

Justine drove him home, made him soup, sent him to bed.

'It's rare to survive a brain haemorrhage, they did

what they could,' she said quietly to him the next evening, dropping in after surgery hours.

He'd found a copy of the consent form, rummaging in her drawer in the night, looking for her mascot, her tiny old teddy bear to clutch. She had signed the form and not told him. Justine had known. She was down as the witness. 'It was your idea,' he accused.

'No.'

'You encouraged her.'

'No, I wouldn't have done that. I asked if you were in agreement.'

'Oh. And what did she say?'

'She said she'd work it out with you, that you'd come round, she knew you would.'

'She was wrong.'

'She was so sure. And there wasn't any hurry, was there.' They stared at each other.

'That she could go ahead and do this when she knew I wasn't happy about it!'

'Ben, I understand your anger.'

'Do you.'

'Écoutes, if it's that dreadful, you can revoke the bequest. It's OK, that's allowed.'

'Is it? Good. But I wouldn't dream of it,' he said savagely. 'It's her body, not mine, her wishes, not mine.'

He choked. 'I thought I knew her. I loved her.'

'And she loved you. You know she did. I'm so sorry. No one could have expected her to die so suddenly, and way before her time.'

'When will they finish with her? When do I get her body for burial?'

Justine shook her head. 'You don't. She'll be cremated by the hospital.' She poured the tea left in his mug into hers and produced a flask from her bag. 'Here.' She poured brandy. 'Drink that.'

Adam had to be told, but every time Ben had tried from Maryann's bedside, he'd got voicemail.

Now he went for the whisky bottle, poured himself a stiff drink. He picked up the phone and tapped the buttons and steeled himself.

This time, at last, the phone was answered.

'Dad.'

'Hello, Adam, it's Dad.'

'Yes, I know.' The abrupt voice grew warm, relaxed. 'It does come up on the screen.' He was laughing.

'How are you?' How silly, Ben thought, to be wasting time like this.

'I'm fine. I'm just back from an away-week, well, an away-five-days. They took our phones and tablets off us.

For the experience, they said.' He was laughing. 'Can you imagine? Five whole days without? Anyway, how are you? How's Mum?'

'I'm. I'm.' He tried again, stalled. Gulped at his glass of whisky. 'Your mother, my lovely Maryann…' His voice trailed away.

'Dad? Is Mum there? Can you put her on?'

Ben took a deep breath, controlled himself. 'Adam, I'm so sorry. Maryann. Your mother. She's dead.'

'I don't believe you.'

'It's true.'

Silence. Ben closed his eyes as he waited.

'Just like that? Was it an accident? Why didn't you let me know?'

'Your phone.' Silence. 'It was sudden,' Ben told him. 'A brain haemorrhage.' He blew his nose, folded the wet cotton, thought distractedly about Adam's teasing, 'Only the over-sixties use handkerchiefs instead of tissues, Dad, and you're not sixty yet. So why are you?'

'I'm coming, Dad. I'll get the next train.'

A howl ripped from Ben's belly as he put down the phone.

'What have you done about the funeral, Dad?' Adam asked, almost the minute he arrived, after they'd hugged. Oh, his son. Practical, like his mother.

Ben shook his head.

'Dad? Funeral?'

'There isn't going to be a funeral. She's been taken away. She wanted her body to be left to the university, of Leeds, as if that matters. For anatomy lessons, and so on. I hate it, but she wanted it.'

'She did?' There was a long pause. 'Oh. Good for her. Well, it is good, isn't it.'

'Have a memorial service,' the vicar urged. 'It will give a sense of closure.' Maryann's uncle, Max, had driven south to fetch Ben's mother. She, once in Settle with Ben and Adam, was organizing things from her wheelchair, and she'd asked the vicar to call.

The vicar must have caught the look on Ben's face, and had the grace to look embarrassed. 'In a manner of speaking, closure. Well, at any rate, a service would help, believe me. Besides, what about your son, what about Adam here? What about her parents?'

'They're both dead.'

A pause. 'Well, your mother then, her uncle. Her friends, the people who knew her.'

'She won't be there! She'll be lying somewhere on a cold slab, or worse.' His voice was raw.

'My darling, you must do something, the vicar's right,' said his mother, 'isn't he?' she appealed to Max.

Ben conceded; he tried to believe them all. He arranged the service numbly, with their help and the vicar's, choosing the hymns he thought Maryann would like, would have liked. Left to himself he wouldn't have had the service, one in his Maryann's memory, not without a coffin and her inside. 'People won't know the half of her,' he said to the vicar.

'So tell them.'

He couldn't. Adam tried, did his best to capture what she was, what she had been. But Adam hadn't known her as long as Ben. Max had, and so had Ben's mother, and so had Justine and Harry, Katie and Tim, and Becky. But that was different. No one knew her intimately. Only he knew her dreams, her dreads. Only he could carry those now, he alone.

The service came and went. He was numb. He stayed numb. Afterwards, when he stopped listening in the pub to people telling him their stories, speaking words of comfort, doing their best, he left everyone there and went back to the churchyard and wandered about. All the names on the gravestones and none would be hers. He wept then.

Fifteen

A letter came in the post, her writing on the envelope, and his heart leapt. They always wrote to each other when separated, proper letters that you could carry around. She wasn't dead at all, he'd imagined it. She was alive. He turned it over to slit it open. 'Delayed for two weeks for lack of the correct postage,' it said.

My darling,

There's a river at the bottom of Becky's land. I take off all my clothes and step into the water, down on to a stone shelf, shivering a bit because it's early morning, and the others are sleeping, except Becky of course who's somewhere around the farm. With the next step, my foot doesn't touch anything so I let my body fall forwards into the water. I think the bottom's quite muddy because I can't see anything down there, just my hands and arms as I swim, turned golden from the peat in the water. Some comes in my mouth. It tastes clear, and a bit sweet. I swim to a shallow waterfall across the top of my pool, falling from a wide rock shelf. It goes across the width of two rocks. So that's one boundary. Then there's one sloping bank of the river where black limousin cows are grazing, and the other bank behind where I shed my clothes, where a couple of trees grow crookedly over the water, their roots partly exposed. And at the end, there's the row of rocks where I got in. That's the pool. There's no one around. It's just me.

Becky says we must come and stay a few days, the two of us. We could help her, too. She could have done with help this year sewing up the wool bags once the sheep were sheared, she says. Next summer. But any time. Let's take a decent break, we've both been working too hard, you for your exhibition, me obsessed by my research, especially by that woman. It's been as if she's a parasite, burrowing into my mind. When I come back, we'll make up for it, I promise. I love you.

Always your Maryann

He felt as though he was losing his mind. He had a gin and tonic, and another, a few more. They gave him a three-day headache.

Becky rang. He cut her off in mid-flow. She rang again, and again. And it was always the same. 'Sorry, I have to go,' he'd say.

Down at the river, a couple of flowerpot men lay bedraggled in a heap, like collapsed string puppets. Some joker had erected a wooden cross, one chunk tied roughly to the other with string, and on the horizontal, R on the left and IP on the right.

Standing over them was Max, his lurcher on a lead. Ben stopped beside him.

'Look at the two of us, honouring these things in respectful silence,' Max said at last. 'How are you, Ben.'

'Oh … you know. Fine. Fine.'

'You were much missed at the private view.' Max had gone in Ben's stead to the private viewing of the exhibition that contained his paintings, among others.

Ben grunted. 'It was good of you to go.'

'I've set up a website for my poetry but no one looks at it. Facebook only seems to work if you put up "Plans for today". Not easy, is it. How's the painting going?' He looked searchingly at Ben.

Ben shook his head.

'Ah.' They were quiet. 'Why don't you get a dog, for

company, like? To help meet people, women.'

Ben didn't answer.

'I'm sorry. That was crass of me.' Max paused. 'I was thinking of going to Wakefield to the Hepworth Gallery. You might like to join me.'

Ben didn't feel he could say no. He inclined his head. 'I might.'

He didn't.

Harry dropped in, several times. He took him off for walks; Ben barely spoke.

Another time he drove up with Ben's paintings in the van, just a few. 'The rest were sold,' he said, and received a glimmer of a smile. 'And this guy in Leeds,' he produced a business card, 'would like you to be in touch about an exhibition there. Ring him.'

Ben chucked the card on a pile of papers.

'Justine sends all her love,' Harry said. 'She's feeling bad about witnessing.'

'I can't help that.'

Harry frowned. 'You should get away. Come and stay,' he urged, after a moment's silence. 'Justine is longing to cook you a decent Burgundian meal.'

'I can't. And it's not Justine's fault.'

'You sound so angry.'

He broke down at that. 'Don't you see? Can't you understand? She's not here, Harry. There's no grave, I can't talk to her. I can't even see her in my dreams. Of course I'm angry!'

'You might like to see Maryann's notes, the research she was doing.' Katie brought round an old-fashioned buff folder and handed it to him.

He shook his head, dumped the folder on the low table, beside their cups, there to languish. He'd no desire to see what had fascinated Maryann so.

From a bag Katie produced a homemade loaf of bread. 'I wish you would come over to us at the weekend. You could listen to that jazz of yours with Tim. I bet you're not eating properly. Do come,' she persisted when he didn't agree.

In time, friends avoided him. Or backed off because he was avoiding them. He didn't know which, and didn't care. He knew he was appalling company.

He couldn't paint.

He couldn't cook.

He couldn't concentrate to read.

He couldn't laugh.

He couldn't sleep.

He couldn't sing. He couldn't even weep and wail.

Not enough.

All he could do was walk. That early autumn it rained. It rained without ceasing. It thundered down on the studio skylight, it slid out of full gutters, it dripped from eaves, it sloshed against steps, it draggled the feathers of the chickens on the nearby allotments where they perched, disconsolate, on the rim of their corrugated-iron shelter. It slid like a snake under the kitchen door up to the cooker and rested there. It rose like smoke from the road outside and carved out rivulets in the earthen drive. The sky wept.

Ben pulled on wellies, his oilskin, so old that it was almost mossy, and the sou'wester that Maryann had bought him, infuriated at his obstinacy at wearing wool in deep rain, and he went out.

'If this were snow,' a neighbour said, walking her miniature dogs, their tummies brushing long wet grass, eyes reproachful under sodden fringes, 'it would be thick and glorious.'

'Bit early for snow,' grunted Ben. He crossed the green and set off up the steep narrow road, through streams of water coming down, past the farm, sheep in the field beside, huddled miserably against the wall, and off to the right, through the five-bar gate, stiff and swollen. Galloway bullocks in the hollow, coats drenched, walked then trotted up and away from him and re-gathered, staring dispassionately down at him as he slithered and slid below, along the churned-up mud from their hooves, beside the stone wall to the next gate.

The gate swung open. As he turned to close it, he stopped. He didn't remember opening it. He hated this. Since Maryann's death he frequently had no recollection of an action just performed. He pulled it back to close, fastening it, before setting off walking up the steep side of the moor. He stopped to look down at the town and the allotments, but a curtain of fresh rain drove towards him, obliterating the view.

'I go on your walk now,' he whispered. 'This was your walk!' he said loudly. He brushed water from his eyebrows and looked down at his hand, curled loosely at his side as if wanting to hold another's, lonely now, empty. 'Why have you left me?' he shouted into the mist, looking round as though she would suddenly materialize. 'Why won't you even show me your face in a dream? I don't understand.' Only twice had he dreamt her, at least he thought it was her, but each time she was moving away from him, always against the folds of a moor. 'Never mind,' he tried comforting himself as he concentrated on not sliding sideways down the wet grass.

He scrambled over the stone stile at the top, and over the second and, a sodden moor later, over the wooden ladder, slippery from its soaking, and back down the lane, Settle invisible below in cloud, or was it the rain in his eyes. Instead of turning home, he went on down to the Lion, hoping that the fire in the pub would be lit, unlike the cold hearth at home.

Hanging sodden coat on the coat rack, picking up a newspaper on the way, he ordered coffee and went to sit at the blazing log fire. He left the coffee on the table, untouched, the newspaper unread and walked out. Back at the house, there was a note on the table from a neighbour, he didn't know who, didn't recognize the writing: 'Your supper's in the oven.' He turned off the light and lit candles, as they had done over supper, and ate what was in the casserole, tears trickling down his cheeks and into the food.

Sixteen

Weeks came and went. Ben would jerk awake in the middle of the night, as if roused by someone or something but there was no one there.

A letter came from the University of Leeds inviting him to the annual memorial service for the bodies left there for cutting up. He didn't answer it. People were kind to him. They persevered. They asked him over for tea or coffee, they suggested he join their choir, they told him he still needed time. Once Max came and virtually strong-armed him into going to the pub. He left early.

And then it was two days off Christmas.

'Dad.'

'Son.' They embraced at the door.

'I see you put up Mum's wreath,' Adam said, ducking under the lintel as he entered through the front door, suitcase in one hand and a bulging carrier bag in the other containing, so far as Ben could see, packets and expensive-looking food.

'Your mother would be cross if I hadn't.'

'She would. But Dad,' Adam was looking around the dining room with its large old fireplace. 'No tree?'

'Do you mind?' Ben didn't wait to hear his answer. He'd gone on through to the drawing room. 'The fire's lit. What'll you have to drink?' he called over his shoulder. 'Beer? Gin? Wine? Whisky?'

'Wine, please. Red, if it's open. I'll go and dump these,' he held them up. 'But really: no tree?'

'Well, it's not as if you're here for Christmas Day. Which is fine, you know it is,' he said quickly. 'It was your mother who was always so keen on Christmas. So... ' he trailed off.

Ben was halfway through a glass of wine by the time Adam reappeared 'Sorry about that. I had a call. Is that mine?' He took the glass. 'Cheers.'

'Cheers.'

They sat in silence. Ben didn't know what to say. Maryann would have known. If she'd been there. But she wasn't, which was the point, wasn't it. Adam tossed a log on the fire and it flared up. The only sound in the room now was its crackle and roar.

'What's on the menu for tonight? Anything special?' A cock crowed in the room. 'Sorry, Dad. Must take that,' as he pulled out his phone and cut off the crowing. 'Hello, my love.'

Ben glanced over. Adam's face was softening, tender with love as he listened. He was glad for his son. But, truth be told, envious, too.

'I'll take it upstairs,' Adam mouthed at him.

Ben sighed. He'd almost finished a second glass before Adam reappeared.

'I'm sorry. I've turned off the phone and left it upstairs. No more interruptions, I promise. Listen, Dad. I've brought food, we can have that.'

'I put potatoes in the oven to bake,' Ben said defensively.

'Fine, we'll have those too, and tomorrow I'm taking you out. And in the morning we'll see if we can find a tree. There'll be one somewhere; we've two days to go till Christmas, after all. What's this?' He'd picked up the folder of Maryann's notes.

'Oh, that. Katie brought it round. It's stuff your mother was working on.'

Adam opened it and started to read. 'Phew!' he exhaled. 'May I have another glass of wine, Dad?' He read on. 'Listen to this. It's from a journal by a preacher.'

December 31
By the kindness of Mr Hay I have been enabled to visit the huts at Dent Head 6 miles beyond

the Moorcock Inn. It has been a very severe frost for a week past and with the occasional falls of snow it has made bad travelling. Icicles were hanging to Mr Hay's beard.

'Icicles!' Adam flicked over a page or two. 'Listen. Here's an entry two months later:

> February 25
> I have often seen sights in the huts of a very shocking character and did today but as it is an understood thing that what I see in my visits at the huts (whatever I may say to them personally) I forbear to record it here. I can only say it made my heart ache.

'Those were photocopies pasted in,' Adam told him. 'Mum's written stuff below. Look, there.'

Ben snatched it from him, and read the familiar scruffy italic script:

> 'I saw this: I saw a woman, far gone in pregnancy. She was walking a path to her cabin, carefully, so as not to slide on the mud and water that had seeped onto the stepping slabs laid in the bog. She could do

nothing about her skirt, already heavy from mud, laden as she was with potatoes for the little ones and herbs in her other hand, fennel for the colic, and rosemary for energy, and a precious pat of butter that a farmer's wife had given her in exchange for help in churning.

When she got to the door, it was open and he was waiting for her.'

Ben flicked through a few pages, and read some more. 'Dad? Dad? What is it? You look dazed.' Adam came over and took the folder that lay loosely now on Ben's lap. He read on for himself, and then, out loud:

'From where she lay on the floor, curled up in agony, Dinah watched Erin yank on his shirt, his tight knee-breeches and ribbed woollen stockings, damp and muddy still from the day before because she had not dried them for him and the fire was out. "No porridge!" he stormed at her, but how could she have made porridge when she could hardly stand? He left, slamming the door, making the thin timbers of the hut shake.

The children whimpered. Somehow she did force herself to her feet. "Come." She managed to assemble them at the door. "We're going on an adventure." From the jug on the shelf she took coins.'

'Hey, was Mum writing a novel? Did you know?' Adam closed the folder.

Ben shook his head. 'No idea.' He felt exhausted. 'We need food.'

That night, he could not sleep. He came downstairs, chucked a log on the embers and picked up the folder. It fell open just before where he had left off the previous evening, at another pasted-in passage from the preacher's journal.

June 29

A very sad affair has happened to one of our men's wives. She got drunk on the Saturday, and when she got home her husband beat and kicked her in a most brutal manner. She took refuge in another hut over Sunday still suffering greatly from the ill usage. She has six small children and was confined of twins five weeks ago but both died.

Then in Maryann's scrawl:

'Determination led her, aching, stumbling, limping, over the moor and down to the main viaduct workings and the railway halt at Batty Green, the children in tow. Never had it seemed so far. "Where are we going?"

"To Settle," was all she could answer, concentrating on her footsteps, dragging her body along with them, denying the pain. At the halt the conductor helped them onto the train and took most of the precious pennies she proffered.

The Spread Eagle shut their door on her. "You made your bed; you must lie in it."

"You were clean and respectable once," the schoolmaster said when she presented herself at the schoolhouse door. No, she could not return there to teach, and he turned away. His wife, shocked at the state of her clothes and the livid bruising that was visible on her face, agreed to take her in and the children, for old times' sake, just for a couple of days, mind, while Dinah went hunting for work.

No one would employ her. Too muddy, too bruised, too shattered. Desperate, she traipsed up to the top of Settle, to the tannery there on the edge of town.

The overseer refused her. She stood in the yard and begged. She smiled the smile that Erin used to say he liked but her face was crooked from the beating and it came out wrong, and still they wouldn't take her. The tannery owner's wife came out to see what all the fuss was. Dinah wept in front of her. "I'll do anything," she pleaded, "cook, clean, look after your children." The wife glared at her bruises and lifted her chin dismissively. "I need no one, thank you."

"May you meet such a hard heart as you have given me, when you need kindness," Dinah cursed, her voice cracking. "May you and yours after you live here in unease.'"

Tannery: our house? Maryann had scribbled in pencil in the margin.

And then the journal took over from Maryann.

> The man sent for his wife several times. But she would never go back to live with him and said 'she wished God might strike her dead if she returned.'

Shaken, Ben shoved the folder under a pile of old magazines out of sight. He stared out of the window into the darkness, resting his hand on the old stone frame.

Was Maryann right? Could it be here that the woman had come, here where she had been turned away? It was Maryann's invention, surely, just as there was inconsistency between her writing and the journal; the preacher said she'd sought refuge in another hut, which was not what Maryann had written. He poured himself a whisky and went back to the window, wondering.

Over at the stone table where he and Maryann loved to sit for drinks on summer evenings, someone was seated, their back to him, looking out over the moor. Ben raced to the door and yanked it open: 'Maryann!'

The figure half-turned. It rose as Ben was crossing the grass between them. He was rushing, and yet his feet were leaden and would not move as fast as he willed. A few more paces and he would touch her. A bit closer. He stretched out his arms, but before him the shape was blurring and as he stumbled forward all his fingers touched was fine mist. A swirl of breeze hit the skin on the back of his neck. His arms were stretched out into empty darkness.

He retreated to the kitchen, feet icy cold. He locked the door and bolted it, drew the heavy curtains over the window, swigged back the whisky and shivered his way back to bed, there to lie awake.

By the morning of Christmas Eve when Adam came down with his suitcase to leave, Ben felt guilty. 'I've not been good company, have I.'

Adam shook his head. 'You're not the only one who's lost her, you know.'

No, thought Ben. But she has taken our joint memories and our hopes for the future. Maybe she's even taken my soul.

They held each other tightly. 'Happy Christmas,' they reassured each other, and Adam was gone.

On Christmas Day, Ben made an effort and went to church. People came up and talked to him. That was when the shame started. Other people got over it. They were all around if you looked, men and women lost friends and lovers, children lost parents. They got over it.

But throughout those winter months he continued to turn down invitations, not wishing to be a bore. All he wanted was to hear her name, all he wanted was to go to the churchyard and talk to her. He did go. He walked around, examining gravestones, wondering when those beneath had stopped having loved ones to visit, fury rising in him at her refusing to be here. He couldn't plant Lenten lilies on her grave or leave a memento as others had done, two lager cans weighed down with pebbles on a young soldier's grave. She had spoiled that.

One night, in desperation, he got out paper, cut it into pieces, marked the pieces with letters, upturned a glass, lit a candle and turned off the lights, and tried Ouija on his own.

Nothing happened. Except that he knocked over the glass.

He had lost her.

Seventeen

That was the lowest point. Adam was ringing him almost every night. Ben knew he was concerned, and he pretended to be fine, while knowing that Adam knew that he was pretending.

March came and, with it, Maryann's birthday. He had to do something.

Carlisle, he decided. Suddenly he was on his feet and running down the hill; he'd be in time for the midday train if he hurried. He jogged to the end of the platform and crossed the line by the bridge just as the train pulled in. He'd light a candle for Maryann in the cathedral there. He could do that at least.

From the city station, he was blown along the main street in a rising wind, past market stalls bereft of customers, their sides flapping, and on to the sandstone-red cathedral. Inside the great Norman entrance, there was organ music, a phrase being repeated as an organist practised. He checked the noticeboard for services, in case one was about to start and not wishing to intrude, but all was clear for him to wander. He passed tombs of bishops, hands folded in repose. He sat on a stone shelf with his back to the story of St Anthony on medieval painted boards. High windows rattled in the outside wind as if saints were trying to escape their stained-glass eternities. He went on through the carved wooden screen to the body of the cathedral and sat down on a rush seat. The gothically carved dark choir stalls, each seat with its jagged spire, each its own cathedral, led upwards to carved angels that jutted out from the blue and gold ceiling above. The organ music crescendoed from a quiet, simple melody to mighty waves that resounded in the high space, bouncing back, as if aimed at Ben. He felt impelled to sink down, bury his head in his hands, as the chords washed over and around him.

He didn't know how long he stayed there on his knees. Slowly, he became aware of someone beside him. He raised himself and sat back on the chair, blinking a few times to return to where he was, before he turned his head. The dark-robed man beside him rested his hand briefly on Ben's. 'Are you all right?'

Ben took a deep breath and nodded. 'Thank you, yes. My wife . . . Maryann . . .'

'I understand.'

They sat there, side by side. Ben lost all sense of time

again. He was grateful for the priest's silence, and for his company.

'I came to light a candle for her,' he said at last.

'I'll leave you to it,' said the priest. Briefly, he rested his hand on Ben's head. 'God bless you,' and he was gone, with a whisper of fabric.

The peace lasted through the lighting of the candle. The candles had been near the entrance all the time, and he had not seen them.

The peace lasted when he came out and crossed the road to the warren of the second-hand bookshop. He picked out a book of old maps of Asia and sat on the windowsill to study them, places so far away, cup of tea at hand. It lasted all the way back to the station.

Maryann would have laughed at him. 'Why didn't you stay the night at a b & b?' she would have asked. 'What was keeping you? Typical!' But he couldn't. He had to get home. Tears gathered in his eyes and plopped onto the lenses of his glasses. He took them off and wiped his eyes. She would have said he was a skinflint, not staying the night, not extending his treat. Was lighting a candle to his lost love in the cathedral a treat?

Back in the train, he shut his eyes and slept fitfully until Dent Head station. He jolted awake and sat up straighter to look out, past the palisades high above the railway holding back a line of snow not quite melted. High embankment rolled down to streams and tracks, the grass still straw-coloured from the winter cold, but green starting to show through in the dips. Approaching boggy wilderness under dense, deep-green trees up above, he felt a draught in his ear, a puff of air. The windows were closed, sealed tight. He shifted on his seat, glancing sideways at the woman seated beside him but she was impassive, dignified as a judge, looking straight ahead, as they entered the tunnel beneath Blea Moor. She could not possibly have breathed in his ear.

He moved anyway, to a table seat across the aisle. They emerged from the dark tunnel, travelling through a deep cutting. There it came again, a puff in his ear. It was like a breath, like Maryann at night, her head close to his on the pillow, breathing warmly. Except that the breath was not warm.

'Ladies and gentlemen, the train will shortly be arriving at Ribblehead, Ribblehead your next station stop.'

He looked down from the viaduct as the train slowed, saw the track alongside where he had walked that last time with Maryann. A solitary walker now below, staring up at him in the half light.

When Adam came for the weekend, he told him

about going to Carlisle. And then, diffidently, about that breath in his ear.

Adam looked at him in concern. 'I bet it was a draught, Dad. Don't go batty on me, imagining things.'

'I don't think I'm imagining it. You know, your mother once… We were on a walk out of Ribblehead, she-'

'She what, Dad?'

'Nothing.' He waved dismissively.

'Come on, let's go to the pub. You need to get out more.'

Ben didn't point out that it had happened not at home but when he was out. Except, what about the weeping Maryann had said she'd heard, the night he and Harry were away? What about his nightmare race outside, just before Christmas when Adam was asleep in bed? Both incidents had been at home.

Eighteen

Once Adam had gone again, Ben tried going to cafés, no longer easy in the house. You didn't need to talk to people: it helped just to have them around as you ate an eccles cake or a slice of curd tart and read the paper. It's probably to do with blood pressure, Maryann would have teased him. If you're in a room on your own, all you need is for one person to come in and your blood pressure will rise, only slightly, mind, but enough to put you in a different frame of mind. She was always coming out with stuff like that. Correction: she always used to come out with it.

The women at the next table were talking for Yorkshire. 'It'd give him a nosebleed going to Morecambe, it would.'

'Well, someone's got to live there.'

'Aye.' They sighed in unison, stirred sugar in their coffee in unison.

He opened the folder he'd brought with him. He hadn't touched it since Christmas but now that the days were lengthening, now that he was out of the house, it could be easier to read. There were only a couple of pages left. In Maryann's writing, he read:

'Dinah's cheeks were being slapped, one side then the other.

She was dizzy, felt as light as a curlew's feather. When she opened her eyes, she saw the schoolmaster's wife peering down at her. "You were having a fit," she said. "Come, lean on me."

Three days later, it was different. "How long will you disobey your husband? It is twice he has sent for you. Return to him," she urged. "It is where you are needed. If you do not, it will be the workhouse for you. I have enquired. They have a place. I can look after the little ones."

Dinah stiffened. "I would die there."

"Nonsense. You are young."

"If I died in the workhouse, they would take my body away to cut it up."

The schoolmaster's wife looked away. She, too, had heard the rumours. "Return to your husband," she repeated. "It is your duty."

"I shall send for the children," Dinah said, "when I am settled."

The woman nodded. She took Dinah to the station, bought her a ticket and watched her leave, along with farmers, red-faced and reeling from their day at market.

Once out of the train, Dinah limped up through the viaduct-building bustle and banging, through the smoke and soot of the brickworks, the ringing of metal on metal, the explosions from blasting, on up to where the air was clearer. Buzzards mewled above as she lurched from tussock to tussock, skirting the boggy patches where she could, the grass cool on her wet feet. She found a rock where she could sit out of the wind to rest. She picked up a stone that lay between her feet, thinking how like an arrowhead it seemed, and held it pensively as she gnawed the heel of bread and cheese that the schoolmaster's wife had given her. With each mouthful, her spirits lightened a little. Why go back to Erin? She knew how to read and write. The schoolmaster's words had stung. She would be clean and respectable again. She would go to the preacher, in her best dress, and ask for work at the moorland school that he was setting up; there would surely be accommodation attached and she could send for the children. Excited by her plan, she set off again, slipping the arrowhead in her pocket, her limping pace quickening even though she was climbing upwards now towards Dent Head. She jumped across a marshy stream but misjudged its width in her bruised awkwardness, and stumbled. As she righted herself, the world swirled about her and she was falling.'

There Maryann's writing stopped. Below it, she had inserted a line from the journal:

She fell down in a fit and was taken home by some of the men.

Ben frowned. Beside him in the café, he heard, 'He knocked on the door. He said, Oh, I didn't know it was you. I said, well, I didn't know it was you either. And I just stood in the doorway, daft as a brush, not moving. He wanted to know how I'd describe "ironic". Well, I don't know how you'd describe ironic. Do you? Well, so I asked him in …'

The woman's voice babbled up and down, unceasing, from beside him. 'And he said …'

So Dinah had been taken home, back to her husband. End of story. He wanted Maryann, not this woman. He left the café and headed off home, chucked the folder down on the growing pile of papers on the table, dislodging half onto the floor. Dumping them back on the table, a business card fell out for the gallery in Leeds that Max had given him. He'd go, he decided swiftly, get away from the folder. He could at least see what the gallery was like, and it would take him away from the Old Tannery.

At Leeds station, he felt drawn to the nearby river and the path running alongside, away from the crowded, noisy city. There was no hurry to head for the gallery, no one was expecting him. The path led to a footbridge that curved back on the river, leading to the canal. He followed that, too, turning left; there was a lock with a lock-keeper's cottage that wouldn't have looked out of place in the country, but ahead, over a hump-backed bridge, rose tall urban buildings. To their side, Victorian arches beneath the station were filled in by cafés; at the end, one was open, to lead round and back up to the station. Inside, arches stretched away from him, dank and dimly lit, vast cellars that echoed to the rumbling of trains, overlaid by a pounding of water. He followed the noise to a walkway suspended over a torrent; water from the higher river chased down at him and beyond to the canal behind, driven through a tunnel, its stone walls blackened and sinister with age. The water roared at him standing there on the walkway, as if inviting him to fall and join its race. Above it, a ledge hugged the length of wall, blocked off by an iron gate, its spikes sharp. Not once since Maryann's death had he felt moved to sketch, yet now, feeling a spark of interest, he concentrated, fixing the scene in his mind.

As he did so, a word rushed at him over the water, 'Find', and another word that he couldn't make out. 'Find,' came again, insistent. Giddy, he clutched the iron rail, not wanting to be pulled into the churning water below. He dragged his eyes away and strode down the walkway to firmer, tarmacked ground, barely registering the cars parked under naked lightbulbs inside separate arches, like something out of an Edward Hopper painting.

'Find.' It reminded him of something. He stopped. A young man cannoned into him. 'Sorry,' he muttered, trying to grasp the wisp of memory, and failing.

He hurried home to the Old Tannery. There the folder lay, as if alive. He flicked through it to the end, saw on the reverse of the last page, one last photocopied piece. A Journal entry from mid-September:

September 13

One of the men was found dead in bed. He had
been drinking since Saturday night, went to bed
drunk and never woke again. I visited the poor
widow today and, as might be expected, she was
in deep trouble.

He sat down and leaned back, closed his eyes,
drained of the strength to make any sort of movement.
Sleep hit him.

That was when the dreaming started, the haunting.

Dinah's neighbour Martha had been kind before.
Dinah went to her cabin with a handful of freshly dug
potatoes.

'Come in,' Martha beckoned, 'I was making straight.
Neighbour Jane and Neighbour Agatha are here, too.'
As Dinah greeted them, the hem of her dress caught on
a nail in the door opening and she stumbled. Potatoes
rolled from the basket she was carrying. In trying to stop
them spreading their soil on the newly swept floor, she
knocked against a broom and it fell. Quickly she righted
it; she knew the superstition.

But in the silence that followed, Jane crossed her
index fingers and pointed them at Dinah. 'Evil is come

into this home. We heard about the elf bolt in your pocket when you fell in your witch fit on the moor, oh yes, we heard.'

'And when you came home, you cursed your husband, and he died,' chimed in Agatha, 'and you know more of herbs than is right.'

'The elf bolt was but a sliver of stone, an ancient arrowhead,' Martha chided Jane, 'and with her herbs Dinah cured our Will.' She bent to help pick up the potatoes. But not before Dinah saw a flash of fear, of doubt cross her face, and Agatha and Jane were quick to leave, sidling out of the door like slugs.

And so it started: the name-calling, the not opening of doors to her. She heard the whispers, saw the turning away. She had cursed her husband and he had died. She had lost charge of her children. Always quiet and with no friends, only acquaintances, in her grief she was quite alone.

She retreated inside the cabin. She was silent and sullen when, at the end of the month, the company man came with the overseer, and said she must vacate the premises, she wasn't working for them, was she, and her man was gone. They had to pull her out, she was so obstinate. The overseer hung back, Abraham Loller. She knew him. She begged him for mercy. He shared his bread with her. He took her in among the trees and entered her, stroked away her tears and gave her money. 'I'm sorry,' he said, turning from her. 'I'll come back.'

He did come back, and he was changed. He flung money on the ground between them and followed it with bread. She scrabbled for both. As he watched her tear into the thick crust, his disgust at her and him hissed out. 'You take money. You disgrace me. Filthy slut! Whore!' When he was thoroughly worked up, he knocked her over and raped her. He left her raw. She came to dread his visits, his bringing of food each time he returned, knowing what would follow. He no longer paid her. So it was starve or do it again, with others. Neighbour Wally, for one. He was rough but fast and gave her coins, and, sometimes, a cuddle afterwards, and a drink from his flask which deadened the shame. She crept into a barn to sleep, and when the farmer discovered her he welcomed her for the comforts of her body. As, one night, did his friends. She washed in streams. Her one good dress she hid in the straw. It happened fast, her fall from grace.

Late one afternoon, hungry for different company, desperate at what she had become, she vowed to stop. The preacher had once told her to own her sin. Very well. She was resolved. She would.

She retrieved her dress, unspoiled, untorn, she washed, and she walked to chapel, creeping in at the last. Slowly she relaxed as the attention was not on her but on the preacher, relaxed because she was with others and was safe. In the full chapel, the preacher talked in a quiet voice of drunkenness and debauchery, and his words of salvation that followed were soothing and calming. Abraham Loller was there, his head nodding in agreement with the preacher's words; he was there at the lectern, reading the scriptures; she remembered how he had been that first time. Kind. At the end when they sang 'The long day closes', she wept, for it had been her father's favourite hymn which long ago he had sung to her. Hopeful, her eyes still damp, she lingered outside afterwards, away from the clusters of worshippers. 'I own my sin,' she blurted out as the preacher came up, curious about the new worshipper. 'I have lain with men. I have drunk.'

He waited.

'You will need to make full confession and hold nought back,' he said sternly. 'Will you do that?'

She lifted her eyes from the hem of her skirt. 'I will.'

'Very well. Wait for me, please. I shall not be long. Then I will hear you.'

Dinah was filled with hope. She would tell him

everything, the men she had lain with, even their names, and would not lie with again. She was no whore, nor witch. She would be washed clean in the blood, like he'd said from the pulpit. She would tell him how she could teach and would ask for work at his school. There would be a home again then, and she'd send for her children.

But in the fine, fair evening, the chapel-goers stayed, chatting, and the preacher had things to do and her resolution weakened as she waited. Despair caught her again. A baby, lying on the grass, was wailing, ignored. The blood rushed to her head, she took it up and cuddled it to her, rocking it. The mother, turning, snatched it from her. 'Witch,' she hissed, 'monster.'

Dinah fell, twitching into unconsciousness. When she came round, no one was there but Abraham. The preacher, he told her, had wanted to wait for her, but other, pressing business had claimed him, and he would hear her another day. She was not to lose heart. The preacher had left her in Abraham's care, he the trusted elder. He was to carry her home. His eyes glittered.

He carried her behind a wall, unbuttoned himself, face grim, and used her. She cursed him then through her lonely tears, said she would have him no more. She was going to own her sin. If he did not stop, she flung at him, she would name him. At that, he ripped her dress and her body, and walked away whistling to recover.

Ben, waking, bewildered, didn't know what to make of it. Except that he wanted Maryann to haunt him, but got Dinah. Except that whatever had happened to this Dinah, it had dominated Maryann's life and coloured what had turned out to be their last weeks together.

Where had the weirdness started? That night, he now remembered, with Tim and Katie and Ouija. Ribblehead. He would go there and see what it led to.

Nineteen

Ben drove up the dale, parking outside Ribblehead station. Getting out of the car, he fought the instinct to huddle into his jacket against the blast of wind, and straightened his shoulders as he set off down the stony track. The wind buffeted him forward, setting up wavelets in the puddles in the pitted track. Stunted trees at his side bent in the wind. 'Hello, Munchkin,' he muttered, 'I'm on a mission.' The words swirled into empty air. 'Not many people about. Storm on its way, I reckon.' Not many people? One was all he could see, in dayglo yellow, cycling off into the distance and, nearer the Station Inn, a quad bike with farmer and dog but no sound because the wind was carrying it in the other direction. And a third person, he now saw as he drew closer to the viaduct, a splash of dark blue moving down the path that led from Dent, blue from a cloak, or a billowing skirt, a long skirt.

The wind dropped. Stillness. No sound, not even birdsong. Ben scrunched up his eyes for a better look.

There was nothing to see but an empty path on the moor.

The wind got up again, carrying a whine from the quad bike, behind him now. Such nonsense, he thought, the thudding of his heartbeat slowing to normal. He'd go under the viaduct and follow the track there, see where it led him. He loosened his scarf, letting it flap about him as he passed through the metal gate and on, past the well-kept farmyard and converted barn on the left where Maryann had wanted them to stay with friends and he'd demurred, saying it was too expensive. He stopped now and looked at it, regretting that 'no'. 'We could use it as a base, go for different walks than the usual ones and be all snug in the evenings,' he remembered her enthusing.

In summer when the curlews cried from curved beaks and the grasses grew tall and yellow with buttercups and rust-red sorrel, purple and blue with clover and orchids and speedwell, when thyme scented the rocky parts, the moor was a good place to be, a place that softened the heart in the warmth of the sun.

But now, weeping, stumbling, harsh wind at her back, hinting at the winter to come, mud sucking between her toes, skirt dragging, cold and wet about her legs, Dinah was afraid. No money, no food. To walk on, the only way to keep warm, the only way to keep any spark of hope alive, the only way that something better might come.

She crossed the iron tracks, avoiding the men building a bridge lower down, stone on stone. She stumbled down the embankment towards the stream that led to an ancient bridge and a cluster of small farms; she followed a track, a path, a stile, a track once more, hoping they were leading to Chapel-le-Dale. In the hamlet there she might find work, it was perhaps too far for the witch slander to have reached. At a crossroads, the track ran through a farmyard. The farmer, coming out of a barn, recognized her and drew back but not in time, for she was pleading already, hand outstretched, for 'bread, please, for the love of God, some bread'.

He glanced at the house and pushed her inside. 'Wait,' and he was soon back with bread and a hunk of meat. 'Be gone. Never return.'

She dropped her eyes. He didn't attempt to use her. One night his pleasure, goaded on by others, she was now his shame. She stuffed the food in her pocket and shuffled away.

It was like a film, Ben thought, shown to him alone, and he was in it. And yet it was an illusion. But there, before him, over the stile, was the same farm at the same rough crossroads. His scalp tightened. 'I'm dreaming, Maryann,' he spoke aloud. 'You must have had these dreams, too.'

He went through the farmyard, neither looking to left nor right. He saw no one.

Castles of clouds towered and jostled for space, turning slate grey and dense as the first heavy drops of rain fell. Grimshaw Hall loomed ahead, built into the side of the moor, its stone already darkening, the windows small and mean. Dinah stumbled in her hurry to reach it before the breaking of the storm.

No one seemed to be in the house; no lamplight or candle shone out. She went quietly up to it. A child at an upstairs window in stiff white bonnet, with fierce, piercing eyes, made her jump. Her heart calmed a little when it did not move, and she saw that it was no child, but a doll. But how the doll stared!

She tore her eyes away and peered in at the window. A black dog sprang at her, fangs bared, as if it would tear away the very stones that separated them. She jumped back.

The rain was coming now in fat loud splashes. She hurried away from the window and the door under its ancient date stone. Hugging the wall, she reached a barn and crept into its dry shelter. There was straw here for warmth. She swept armfuls against her and sank down, shivering, against the far wall.

The track led Ben along a scar in the rock, and came to outbuildings and a large house that stood darkly sentinel over the moor, its back against the scar. A handwritten notice told of access to a cave and, if the farmer was out, of leaving a donation.

Ben left some coins under a stone at the door and walked round the house, but found no cave, only the ruin of a small barn, roofless, two windows gaping. Billowing clouds above were folding back in the wind like the duvet on a morning bed, exposing sunshine, and he had an appetite for the apple and cheese and dates in his jacket pocket, so he clambered over fallen stones at the former entrance to the barn and settled himself at the back. Over the crumbling front wall, the trees of the copse swayed in the wind, but here he was sheltered, and so warm in the sunshine that he could take off his jacket. His appetite satisfied, in the peace and seclusion he dozed.

Dinah awoke to men's voices, drawing closer. 'Eh, reckon this could be the place?'

'Not now, lad. To t'churchyard. Parson'll be waiting.'

'Parson won't know.'

A man began whistling.

Dinah stiffened. She hadn't been sure of the voice when it was half-swallowed by the wind, but that whistling she knew and never wanted to hear again. It was growing louder, and with it the sound of heavy boots. She stumbled to her feet, pressing back against the wall, as if she could sink into it and vanish, but it was hard and unyielding. She edged along it, hands outstretched, as the sounds grew ever closer. Then, as if by a miracle, her fingers found air. She twisted round to see a rough gap, and she was through in a flash, her heart thudding. Down to her left the ground dipped and a slab of rock rose, smooth and reaching high into the sky like a chimney stack. 'Rock of ages, cleft for me,' rushed into her mind and as she scrambled down, she grasped the words and melody of the familiar hymn as a lifeline. 'Let me hide myself in thee.' At the base of the dark rock, pale green ferns grew above pillows of darker green moss, all standing guardian to an opening that she now saw in the rock scar at the side. She went in there and crouched.

Ben stirred, uneasy and chilled from his sleep. He put his jacket back on and stood. Now that he was rested, he was keen to find the cave. Close to where he'd been sitting, the wall had crumbled right down to expose an old iron bedstead and bare rock and moor at head height. The land dipped to his left, and that's when he saw a towering rock that he seemed to recognize. Rough steps went down to a cleft in the rock scar of the moor.

Below, it was airless, not a breath of wind, green and moist, and Ben took off his jacket once more and chucked it on the moss at the base of the thickly sprouting ferns and the dark stone rising. To his left a small pond, large enough for a fish, and a trickle of water under his feet. To his right an opening. He was no caver, but this looked safe enough. He reckoned he could explore the first bit. He took his car keys out of his pocket and turned on the tiny beam of light on the keyring.

The whistling was filling the air now. Dinah cowered into the rock, holding her breath in fear. 'Look down here!' she heard a shout. 'This must be the cave they've talked about.'

So he hadn't seen her. She let out her breath, slowly. Other voices joined Abraham's. Dinah moved deeper in, her hands feeling for the walls on either side, fear driving her into the darkness. Here the men would surely not follow her. If they did come, if Abraham came, they would not see her. But if they did come, she would not see them either; it was as black there as the deepest hell. She folded her arms and held herself tightly, swallowing down the acid that rushed into her throat.

But the shouts grew fainter till she could hear them no more. Water under her feet was icy cold. The words from the hymn sounded in her head instead: 'Foul I to the fountain fly; Wash me, Saviour, or I die.'

Twenty

Ben cursed the pinprick of light in his hand. No match for the cave's darkness around, it only lit up the patch he pointed it at, about a foot of rock at a time, and that only faintly. He made out a shallow stream beside the ledge where he walked, close to the wall. He counted his cautious steps, twenty into the cave, twenty-five, and growing colder and clammier all the time.

The tiny battery died. 'Damn.' He turned. No light shone from the entrance behind; the walls must have curved without his realizing. Confused, he turned, and turned back again, his bearings lost, his excitement now edged with fear. He had good night vision but this was like no darkness he had ever known. He'd been foolish to enter, foolish to come unequipped. He was trapped and alone, and the sensations of Dinah in there were strengthening. He could die here and no one would know. Maybe Dinah had. 'Deep breaths,' he muttered to himself, pushing away panic. 'Calm now.' He pressed the keyring again, just in case, and was rewarded with a faint picture before it died for good. The ledge where he'd walked was on his left. 'Now then. You're facing the entrance,' he told himself aloud, for courage, and hoped he was remembering right. 'Put the keys in your pocket so you don't drop them.' He obeyed his own stern words. He walked slowly towards what he believed was the exit, feeling his way with his hands pressed cautiously against the walls on either side. His foot slipped and went into water and he shouted, but it was shallow, no harm done. When daylight showed, he almost cried out in relief. 'Don't hurry,' he told himself, 'take your time.' Outside, in the beautiful green oasis, the shudders came. He pulled on his jacket with shaking fingers, and bent to the thick, cool moss, laying his head on it, as if in prayer.

'Find.' A whisper on the breeze, so faint that he could be imagining it. Yet no breeze could reach down here in the dell, no draught. Like the time before, it felt more like the breath from a human mouth, only cool, not warm. He raised his head and looked round. No one was there.

When she thought she was safe, Dinah crept out and back up to the barn. No whistling could be heard, nor shouting. Careful not to be seen, she peeped out of the window opening in front to see where the men had gone. To her surprise, they were not so very far away, walking slowly, carrying a load, a coffin, she saw, on its way to the churchyard at Chapel-le-Dale where many of the shanty-towners were buried. Abraham Loller was one of the four bearers, Martha's husband another, and Welly. You had to be special to bear a coffin. Parson thought Abraham was special. People thought Abraham special. She knew better. He'd never felt special when pushing her deep into the mud and wet with his thrusts, and battering her, the smell of his guts in her face.

Released from the cave and the crumbling barn, back in sunshine, Ben headed on down the track towards Chapel-le-Dale, over a shallow ford and along an open stretch with broken limestone pavement on either side, following - he was unsure what. He was no longer alone. Hang-gliders, as bright as parrots in their yellow, green and blue, swooped in the sky above, and he stopped to watch, grunting as his skin met a sharp edge of rock, one of more large stones that seemed to have come off a once-sturdy cairn at his side. He sat on a smoother-looking one.

There was a thud, right beside him. He frowned. He surely wasn't that heavy.

Dinah feared that they would tell tales of her in Chapel-le-Dale, would slander her for a witch and a whore, so she followed the men at a distance, confident that she could not be seen, crouching low once she arrived at an open stretch, darting from the shelter of one rock to another.

The men stopped to rest the coffin on a large flat stone, a coffin stone. Rest it on the ground and the spirit of the dead body inside would escape and haunt that place till their dying day, and hers. They stretched their arms, flexed their muscles. Abraham was whistling again, a different tune this time. His companions got out their clay pipes and started tamping them. She leaned against a rock and closed her eyes, she was so tired. She didn't hear the whistling stop.

That's when it happened.

Ben flinched. He wanted to shout out.

Dinah didn't see Abraham circle round to the back of her, she didn't turn in time, didn't see the coffin bearers look up, look her way. The heavy stone that split her skull made her collapse, her breath stop, her heart stop.

The coffin bearers looked away as Abraham dragged

her body to the side. They had known she was there, had known all the time, had known she must not tell, not about them, especially not about their overseer, a man of reputation. Like them. He must not be exposed by that woman. She'd not be missed, not by anyone.

Nor did they help the solitary killer as he got to work. They put away their still-unlit pipes and shouldered the coffin once more and staggered off to Chapel-le-Dale without him.

There on the moor, Abraham stripped her body. He cut her witch's hair, and laid her, curled up, a yard away between two rocks. Grim-faced, he gathered stones and piled them on her. He went further afield, moving swiftly, laid on more till above her in the shape of a cairn was the weight of one man or more.

He put the clothes and hair in a bag, went back to the copse near Grimshaw Hall, took a spade from where it leaned beside the door, dug a hole and buried them. Safe now from Dinah, he stamped hard on the ground to keep them there. When the cur came near, he kicked it away, cursing. The windows looked blankly down.

Ben sat rigid. A wash of undigested dates and cheese rose up into his mouth and out. He wiped his mouth.

He had tried to shout in warning but his teeth had

clamped together. He had tried to run to her but his feet were tied tight to strands of grass.

He screwed up his eyes tightly and opened them again.

Here he was, in sunshine, there were the hang-gliders, swooping still in the windy sky, there the viaduct in the distance. To his left, the way back to Grimshaw Hall, and a glimpse of its roof. To his right, the trees that marked the top of a narrow valley, the track leading down to Chapel-le-Dale.

That night they came back for her. Martha's husband said they could not leave her there, it wasn't right. She ought to be where the other railway workers and their families were buried in Chapel-le-Dale. What, said Abraham, a whore and a witch like her? Besides, she could not be in the churchyard, not without Parson. They argued back and forth. Yet, said Martha's husband, not looking at the overseer, they had done wrong: 'Thou shalt not murder'; nor be a witness and lift no hand to stop it.

They dug a hole for her, not in the churchyard, but close, where the ground was disturbed from the churchyard's recent expansion, on the other side of the churchyard wall in unconsecrated land. No one saw.

There was no one to tell. No one knew, but them.

And Ben. He closed his eyes and circled his head back and round, against an encroaching headache. It felt too real for illusion. As a boy, for a time unhappy and lonely, he had imagined a friend and, later, had found out that the friend had existed, in the past. He could not explain these nightmarish visions, any more than he could have explained what happened in boyhood. He knew though that this story was not finished. He would follow on to Chapel-le-Dale. Now. He got to his feet, and walked away from the gaudy hang-gliders, on to where the track entered trees and dipped steeply, the land becoming pastoral, down to a deep dale, over a bridge and right to the tiny church at the near end of a short street of cottages that petered out into a field.

There were voices coming from the graveyard, and laughter and chat, where he had expected silence. People were digging a shallow trench on the inside of the churchyard wall.

A man saw him and straightened. 'Hullo. Have you come to join our eco-group? We could do with another pair of hands.' He handed him a spade.

Taken by surprise, Ben accepted it.

'You've missed the scything, but you can help dig. It's

for plants that we're putting in along the wall,' the man told him, 'for bees and such. We may not get it done today, mind, we're all a bit zonked from the scything. I don't know about the others, but my shoulder feels wrecked. Lack of experience, I dare say. At least we got the grass cleared.'

Ben helped. He left when they left, the job as yet unfinished. He had barely spoken; he hadn't needed to, since the man had kept up a running soundtrack to the thoughts and dread jostling in Ben's mind. Dinah had been murdered. Dinah had been laid to rest, just the other side of the wall.

It took an hour's brisk walking to get back to the car; only an hour, in which so much had happened on the way.

Twenty-one

Once home, Ben took a beer outside and sat, but couldn't settle.

He closed his eyes, 'Maryann? Munchkin?' trying to summon up her face, but could not. He was frightened that he was forgetting what she had looked like, that only photographs now would tell him. He opened his eyes and went indoors to fetch a book, but he couldn't settle. He went back indoors for the potato and couple of lamb chops he'd put in the oven, and picked watercress from the stream at his side to go with it, and ate it but barely tasted it, and still he couldn't settle.

He took a couple of paracetamols and went to bed. He felt drained, and yet the pounding in his chest and in his neck went on and wouldn't let him sleep.

At one o'clock, he gave in and got dressed again. He fetched a spade and a cardboard box from the shed, and drove direct to Chapel-le-Dale, passing only one car on the way. He parked near the pub on the hill a half-mile outside the hamlet, to be sure that no one would notice and remember the car, and walked down to the church. No window opened nor voice challenged him as he walked round to the outside of the churchyard wall. Slowly he followed the wall.

He stopped. He turned full circle, slowly, listening, alert. He began to dig, sure of the place.

His spade struck something that was less giving than earth. He bent and lifted it out, but it was a stone. Anyway, his digging was still too shallow. He threw it aside and dug deeper, tossing his jacket and then his jumper out on the grass at the edge as he climbed into the pit he was making. He dug on, beginning to doubt, yet using the spade more cautiously now that he was standing up to his chest. The spade touched something hard again, and he bent to it. This time it was bone.

He reached up for the torch and in its flash he saw more paleness showing through the earth. He threw the spade up and scrabbled around with bare hands, carefully lifting each bone in turn onto the grass, till he reckoned he had them all. Then he hauled himself out of the pit and gently laid the bones in the box before filling in the hole, adding heavy stones at the last to disguise the digging.

Now that he had Dinah's bones, he was unsure what to do with them. He couldn't leave them here in a box.

He could take them back with him to the Old Tannery, and that would lift the curse. Or was it already lifted? How could he know? He wasn't used to such ways of thinking.

He was off the grass and walking up the road towards the car, box in arms, spade awkwardly over his shoulder, before he stopped. He turned back.

He leaned the spade at the churchyard gate for ease of movement and went into the graveyard, picking his way through the graves to the wall, to where he had been digging that afternoon, right on the other side of the wall from where Dinah had been buried. He set down the box before going back for the spade, and began to dig again. Gently now, he took the bones from the box and laid them to rest, carefully placing the skull at the last, facing east as in the other graves. At his side, a lavender bush had already been planted. In the church porch were more plants: lavender, sage, rosemary. Rosemary for remembrance. If Maryann had had a coffin, he'd have dropped flowers onto it. If she'd had a grave, he'd have planted flowers on top.

He planted the rosemary now over Dinah's bones, heeling the soil in well.

He bowed his head. 'Be at peace. Rest now.'

Twenty-two

Ben didn't go back to bed that night. He could not, he was too light and giddy, awed at what he had seen, at what he had felt, at what he had done. Bed would be too prosaic, and besides, he knew he would not sleep. He drove up near Ribblehead station and started to walk back towards home. He could come up later by train to fetch the car.

It was a familiar walk, a favourite of his and Maryann's, from Ribblehead, skirting Selside and on to Horton before continuing on home. On the shelving moor over the village of Horton, he stopped in the dark, alone in the company of large and incurious bullocks, to wait and watch for the dawn.

Even after dawn had risen, even after the sun's rays hit the slope of Pen-y-Ghent, turning it golden-pink, he sat there. He sat on until the clouds formed a bank and rolled over the peak, threatening rain, and his stomach cramped for want of food.

He went on down then to the village. He was still too

early for the café, but someone else was an early riser for the church was open and he wandered about there in the dry, before returning to the café in gathering rain. He ordered the first thing he saw on the counter, and sat while they brought it to him, along with a family-sized cafetière of coffee and hot milk. The young owner lent him his newspaper, but Ben was too spacey to read and simply sat there, feeling the goodness of the food and the hot drink slide inside as the rain tumbled down outside.

A gaggle of walkers came in, stripping off dripping layers to emerge drier from their cocoons. Behind them, a woman with a bounce in her walk and red curly hair going grey that tumbled to her shoulders. She smiled at Ben.

He blinked and looked again to see properly.

It had been Maryann.

'Ooh, chorley cakes! Haven't had one of them in years,' one of the group said, squeezing past. Ben lowered the hand he'd raised to greet the vision of Maryann he'd seen behind the newcomers. 'Isn't it cosy in here.'

'Are you going up Pen-y-Ghent?' the woman at the counter asked them.

'I think that's the idea.'

'It'll be slippy, mind.'

'Wouldn't catch me going up there,' called a young man from a further table, 'day like this.'

Rain splashed in the puddles outside. Wind sent twigs from a bush tapping against the window. It was peaceful in there, no music, and warm enough too, and no one looked miserable. Ben gulped at his coffee, almost scalding the back of his throat.

The village church had been cold as death, and yet welcoming, well-polished. He imagined a small congregation of a Sunday, relishing the magic and mystery of the words of the Book of Common Prayer, toughly inured to the chill, and wondered if any parents from the two-room village school brought their children there, or would they be at football or, heaven help us, shopping.

'Don't rant!' Maryann would have said.

'All right, all right.' He lifted a hand, and quickly lowered it as the couple at the next table looked questioningly at him. 'Sorry.' He took the last bites of his chorley cake, the melted butter almost hard by now.

'Two sausage sandwiches.' The woman carried them over to the couple, setting his mouth watering. Decent chunky bread, good butcher's sausages. 'I'll have one of those, too, please,' Ben said, signalling to her.

'Getting your appetite back then?' came a whisper in Ben's ear. A slow smile spread across his face. He reached up to touch Maryann and something seemed to brush his hand.

Twenty-three

The nightmares stopped.

Shaving in the morning, thinking about the day ahead, Maryann's voice would come to Ben. Walking in the afternoons, he would sense her presence. At night, he sometimes saw her in his dreaming, and was comforted.

He rang Katie and sat in a pub with her and told her all he knew about Maryann's work on Dinah, adding quite a bit that he knew himself but careful not to include all that he had done. When, later, Tim joined them, Ben didn't rush off.

He went round to Justine and Harry and apologized for his distance and they hugged him and said no need, and he stayed to eat. When his mother rang, or Adam, he did not put down the phone after only a few minutes, cutting off the conversation. When the invitation came again from the School of Medicine to the Memorial Service on 21 October, he went, and Justine and Harry and Max with him. The Great Hall was full; relatives were there and respectful medical students filed in, too. Some spoke and played music, witnessing to the generosity of the dead. The service was thoughtful, but little of it seemed to touch him; he was more conscious of the sweat gathering in his armpits from the heating. Maryann Waugh, he heard, the name sounding between Stanley Waterhouse and Colin Cadwaladr Williams. But she wasn't there.

After the service they left him in town in the rain as he asked; yes, he was fine, he said, and meant it. He stood for a moment, irresolute, in a shop doorway, hands in his pockets. Shoppers passed on the slick, wet pavement, most with their heads down against the driving wet.

Out of the corner of his eye he saw a young woman detach her hand from the man at her side and stoop to the pavement. She caught Ben's eye, deliberately, it seemed, as she straightened and came over, hand outstretched. Instinctively, he raised his to meet hers. With a smile, she dropped a small silver coin into his palm. 'This is good luck, from me to you.' She rejoined her boyfriend and was away before he had even said a startled thank-you.

He went then to the Taylor Gallery, to discuss a next show, he told them. Scenes from a walk, he said, starting at the Dark Arches here in Leeds and ending in a country graveyard. Trust me. They would, they said, it's been too long, and a deadline was fixed.

Postscript

Samhain, when the ancients believed that the membrane separating those in the present and those in the past was at its thinnest. Samhain, when it was possible for each to pass through, and some did. Taken by the Church and re-christened Hallowe'en, the eve of All Hallows, for all the saints, those who lacked their own saint's day in the church calendar, anonymous souls, except to God.

When Ben awoke on the eve of All Hallows, he prepared bread, for the first time in months, and left it to rise. Sunshine was promised, but not yet, the clouds still low, yet lightening. He went to his studio, took fresh paper and a stick of charcoal, to work on the scene of the moor in late autumn: the outcrops, a cairn, uneven tufts of grass, stones. His movements were swift and sure; he drew and he smudged, till he felt that he'd done justice to it, pausing only to return to the kitchen to knead the dough and bake it.

As the light in the studio started to fade, he looked

out. He threw on a coat and got in the car.

No one living was in the churchyard when he entered: no one but himself, with candle and bread and wine.

He lit the candle beside the rosemary bush that he had planted. He tore a chunk off the loaf in his arms and placed it under the plant. From his bag, he took out the bottle of wine and filled a glass and stood in reflection. He tore off bread for himself and chewed it slowly, gazing down at the grave he had made, and raising his eyes to the moor behind and the sky. He filled his glass and drank. He drank to Dinah. He drank to Maryann.

He poured the rest of the wine onto the grave in libation. He felt an immense sense of lightness. 'I shall be back,' he promised. 'Rest in peace,' he blessed.

On returning, he parked the car at home and walked down the hill to the Lion for a quiet pint. Strains of guitar and fiddle filtered through as he stood in the entrance. In the side room were ten or so musicians. One led, the others followed; one sang, the others accompanied; another led, they listened and followed, melancholy ballad succeeding joyful foot-tapping music that almost had him wanting to dance as he edged his way to the far empty corner and sat back. He'd passed a young woman, and he looked at her now, on the settle. Shortish, dark-haired with a fringe, sipping her wine, reading the paper, seemingly oblivious to the music. Waiting for someone, he supposed. She was demure, French-looking in a dark dress with a white collar. He liked the way it hugged her curves. He wondered about going over and asking if she'd like to join him for a fresh glass of wine.

He smiled ruefully. It was the first time he'd felt so much as a prickle of attraction to a woman.

'The night I fell in love with my Maryann was just such a night in a pub,' he found himself telling the man sitting alongside, 'only without the music.' The man didn't seem to hear him over the sound of a banjo.

No matter. Ben smiled and shut his eyes, dabbing the corners with his fingers to stop any tears leaking through.

Acknowledgements

I am most grateful to the Settle Public Library, to Anne Read of The Folly for access to some of the books below and others, unmentioned but useful for pointing the way. I should also like to thank the Lion and Gladstone's Library for hospitality as well as Jonathan Athay and Cheryl Wood. I consulted the following books:

Byng's Tours, The Journals of the Hon. John Byng, 1781-92, ed. David Souden, Century Books, 1991

W. Henderson's *Folklore of the Northern Counties of England and the Borders*, The Folklore Society, 1878

Frederick W. Houghton and W. Hubert Foster's *The Story of the Settle-Carlisle Line*, British Railway Books, 1965

W.R. Mitchell's *Shanty Life on the Settle-Carlisle Railway*, rev. edn. 2004, Castleberg

And also the blog by Stephen Oldfield on Bruntscar Cave, to which Jess Hart directed me.

I am particularly grateful to Mark Rand for alerting me to the unpublished manuscript in his possession, *The Journal of*

William Fletcher, railway missionary to the workmen on the Settle & Carlisle Line, second contract, transposed and compiled by Kay Gordon, from which I gleaned much detail, including the story of the woman whose life and death I have somewhat embroidered from the sketches in the manuscript. It is now in the possession of the Friends of the Settle & Carlisle Line in Settle. Although I have taken liberties with the material, it remains true in essence to the original. I particularly borrowed the entry for Saturday, 29 June 1872.

Equal thanks are due to Mrs Sarah Wilson of the School of Medicine at the University of Leeds for her kindness and generosity in helping me solve a conundrum or two, and for permission to quote from the School's *Bequest and Information* booklet.

Margaret Rhodes, in Socratean dialogue, helped to resolve a graveyard problem, and Stephen Dawson confirmed the resolution we reached. Helen Woodcock copy-edited the manuscript. Chris Burgon and Helen Stockton designed the book.

The title Stone on Stone is borrowed from a song of that name by The Moonbeams, the Long Preston folk group.

My gratitude is due too to Carol Ann Lee and Maydo Kooy for invaluable criticism, and, especially, to Roger Taylor. Always too my gratitude to Paul Clark, for encouragement beyond measure.

and a taster for the next book . . .

The Flower Meadows

As I joined the s-shaped queue that slunk towards airport security, and slid my small brown leather suitcase forward, one foot at a time, I relaxed. The case, I was told, was as old-fashioned as my name, Eliza; everyone else had wheelies, even when their bags were small. I was fond of the case, had bought it on a trip to China the year before. People commented on it too, mainly people in trains; it was useful, a way of meeting strangers. Besides, I was good at travelling light. Jack and I were both good at that. Jack had been good at that.

I approached the counter and shrugged off my coat into a grey tray on the assembly line; my suitcase I hefted into the next. 'Good morning,' I greeted the security officer, his hands sheathed in blue plastic gloves. He returned the greeting with a surly grunt: 'Keys?' 'In there,' I nodded. 'Mobile phone? Laptop?' I had neither, and shook my head. Who would ring me anyway?

I waited before the metal doorway, watching for the traffic

light to turn to green so that I could go through. My heart was thudding in my throat. Had I been a lizard they would have seen the fierce pulse. I'd quite like to have been a lizard, darting about the place catching flies, sunning myself on stones, slinky. Instead of being ripe and rounded. Not true. Ripe and rounded like a plum was when I was young; at least, that was how Jack had called me. I knew that a stranger looking at me now would see someone motherly, upholstered, even; my hair was fun, mind, short and spiky with a rash splash of mauve, probably too young in style for my sixty-six years, but who cared.

The light on the doorway switched to green. Go.

The doorway buzzed as I passed through. 'Would you step aside, please?'

The queue behind me built up as they waited for a female security officer. I stood patiently before saying that I really had no problem with a man, none whatsoever, and look at the delay behind. A male security officer, conceding, approached and asked me to hold my hands out from my side. I did so willingly. His hands ran over my body and my body warmed to the touch: front, back, along the arms, quickly at the crotch. I was smiling, my eyes closed, relishing the moment.

'Would you empty that pocket, please?' the man asked, pointing to the one over my left breast.

I took out the flat green brooch, a present from Jack, made by a Swedish sculptor friend years ago, that I'd carefully placed there before leaving the house.

An electronic arm swished over me. 'Fine. You may go. Next!'

'Batty!' I heard behind me, and could imagine the head-shaking. I passed on serenely.

Hands had touched me; hands had stroked my body, just. It was going to be a good day. This was what made airports special for me now. The physical, human contact.

The thing is - well, Jack died. That's the truth of it, the beginning and the end, the fact and the dream. We lived in a beautiful place, a place whose little toenail this airport building could not even lick; they were on different planets. It was a gem of a village. Its roads were cobbled and winding and quiet, the people, including us, of course, friendly. There were no polished 4x4s, high off the road with bull bars for bulls that never strayed on to roads, only ordinary mud-spattered Land Rovers, ordinary rusting tractors, ordinary cars for ordinary, special people. Ancient stone houses and cottages, some, like ours, leaning in towards the church that squatted on a knoll in the plumb centre of the village. Bell-ringing practice on Wednesday nights at the church could sound drunken; but then, if you don't like bell-ringing, don't go to live in a village. In June we would wander along the river in balmy sunshine (yes, I admit, not every summer's evening was balmy, but some were; other times, the path was so muddy and slippery that you'd regret coming out, but it's the fine evenings I remember). 'Will the summer come back?' I'd sometimes asked plaintively when sunshine had stayed away a little while. 'Aye, there's no harm in hoping,' Jack would answer, and of course summer did return and Jack and I would walk hand in hand with the river on one side, hay meadows on the other. The meadows were a sheet of tall yellow buttercups, tinged green and silver with grasses, rust-red with sorrel. When you looked closely you saw blue, too, the blue of speedwell, pink and purple of clover and white of daisies. At the stone bridge beyond, bluebells and forget-me-nots coloured the crack where wall met road; and from drystone walls, valerian stretched out its deep pinks to brush our arms; and on the surrounding moors there'd be purple splash of orchid, or yellow swathe of cowslip. One year, the winter feed from the mown meadows was so rich that many sheep bore quadruplets and could not feed all the lambs themselves; two farmers, weary from bottle-feeding so many lambs, invested in a suckling machine to solve the problem. Holiday makers, campers mainly, came to the village and said they never wanted to leave. But they did, and in winter it was left to us and the ghosts of the past whose clicking needles were said to have been heard as far away as Kendal.

All right then. It was Dent. Now I wish I hadn't said that because you'll all go there and it'll get crowded and it won't be mine.

Jack died. I didn't think I could bear to live there without him. We had been sufficient unto one another. Apart from Jasmine, our daughter, that is. She had left Dent at the earliest opportunity for university, for a high-flying career in law. She'd wanted to see the world. What she saw was the view from a smart housing estate and the train that took her to the city. 'Come,' she begged, 'We need you. Now Dad's gone, you can come and be a granny, can't you? You said you wanted to see more of Dominic.' She was right. I had. And I felt selfish even hesitating.

I left Jack's grave to the tender care of neighbours. I sold our much-loved house and moved way south. Foolishly, I left.

A proper granny. That's what I became. I threw myself into it. Little Dominic did need me now that Jasmine was free to work full-time. Jeff was a lawyer, too, and sure and confident in himself; he'd swept Jasmine off her feet, she'd told me, not avoiding the cliché. I'd collect Dominic from playgroup, and later, from primary school and play with him; I took him on outings that they couldn't take him on; I went to his prize-givings, I encouraged his scramblings up on my lap and his cuddles, sticky hands in my hair when he was very small (that was before I cut it really short). I bought a red-brick, newish house in their red-brick newish estate with its 4x4s at the doors and its strimmers strident on summer afternoons that drowned out the drone of bees. My Jack would never use a strimmer. We'd get down on hands and knees, he and I, for the first cut of the year when the gold of dandelions had turned to puff and seed, down on our knees to cut the grass with shears. After that first cut, it was a second-hand lawn mower with that rattling purr that cut the grass when you pushed it. Jasmine and Jeff's place had a lawn, striped, with flowers cultivated and mail-ordered planted neatly at the side, and Jeff would sit on a machine the size of a golf buggy to mow the lawn, up and down, and use the strimmer for the edges so that it never strayed from neatness, tidiness, control.

I love Jasmine, loved her. And Dominic. I understood that Jeff represented something to Jasmine that was apart from me, and Jack. I did my best to love Jeff, or at least respect him, and perhaps he did me, but our wary dislike was mutual. It wasn't his fault. We were different. 'Your mother!' I'd hear him explode upstairs in their bedroom when I was downstairs playing on hands and knees on the carpet with their energetic son, and he'd go on shouting but his shouts would become muffled as their door was closed and the row continued. Afterwards, Jasmine, ever the peacemaker, would come down and ask if I would just sometimes please watch television with Dominic. I meant to, I could see that it mattered to them, but there was always something else that Dominic and I wanted to do first: make paintings from potato cuts, cutting the potatoes first and making a mess with poster paint; or working on a puppet theatre and a show, or reading a book together, or making a jungle of my garden down the road.

It wasn't Jeff's fault when Jasmine was killed in a car crash. Outright. He was driving. The police said it wasn't his fault and so did the coroner, and so did I. He was distraught, his eyes red and tired for days, his hair unkempt. But he had to go back to work. He let Dominic come and stay with me on the nights when he had a woman over, sometimes one from the office, sometimes someone he'd met on the internet. One of them, Elly, he fell in love with. Elly was pleasant enough. Kind, too, to Dominic, I could see that. She didn't like living in the house that Jeff had shared with Jasmine, and who could blame her.

They moved. He forgot to leave me the address. He said that Dominic now had a mother whose work was home-based - and if she decided to go out to work instead, well, they'd get a nanny - so I was no longer needed. I had been a problem, he spat at me. My mess of a garden embarrassed him with the neighbours. I let Dominic out to play, unsupervised; I didn't clean him up when he was grubby. What was worse was my lack of television, and the way I kept the smart phone he had got Jasmine to give me turned off and in a drawer. How could Dominic make friends if he couldn't discuss the latest TV programmes? And what harm would it have done to have taken him for a Big Mac once a week? How was Dominic expected to fit into modern life, let alone become a success when he grew up? I was complicating his little life.

I could see Jeff's point. But I wished I had the address that he never gave me. His parting shot, when Dominic and Elly were not around, was to call me a witch.

I was shocked at their leaving. In despair, I went to church. It wasn't very local, and the hymns in the square building were unfamiliar: songs, they called them, with choruses in odd places and amplified bands. The vicar, a kind woman, seeing me looking lost, I suppose, introduced me to women, more or less my age. They perched on high-heeled, strappy shoes, carried shiny handbags and were trussed in careful hairdos. They had a group, for consciousness-raising, they told me, would I like to join them? They were kind. I feared that my consciousness was already raised too high for my own good, and I declined.

I was lonely. Of course I was. So would you have been. I had to stay there on the estate because that was the only address that Dominic would know when he wanted to get in touch.

I began to look at men with new eyes, trying to imagine

them as a husband, as a replacement for Jack - no, not as a replacement, no one could be that, but as a new companion. It was difficult. Except for the once. I had driven to a park, an approximation of countryside with patches left unmown, a small river, that sort of thing, and a café you could grow fond of. A man stopped me and asked the way to - oh, I don't remember now where to. I couldn't let the moment go; I knew in my belly that he was a man I could live with, just as I had known with Jack when we had first met. When the man had passed, I ran after him, 'hello, excuse me,' and scribbled my telephone number on an old train ticket and gave it to him; ring me, I said. It was batty of me, I know it was, but how could I not act when I knew he and I would be right? He didn't ring. Of course he didn't. Who can blame him. Besides, it was all very well thinking of companionship but what about the physical side of things? Jack and I knew each other's bodies; we had grown middle-aged together, would have grown old together. But a new man? How would he look on this ageing body of mine?

And so, after a while, I decided to escape the house. I sought out distraction. I visited cities with medieval cathedrals, I went to London for the museums, I visited famous gardens. I didn't stay away long, one night, sometimes two; I didn't want to miss a note from Elly about young Dominic, although, she and Jeff might have broken up, you never know. I didn't think Jeff would be in touch. But I hoped for a postcard from Dominic. The trips lengthened. I made acquaintances on my travels but we don't stay in touch.

I went for longer stays, to Europe. I went to La Fenice to see La Traviata, I went to the Alhambra, I travelled north to Finland and prayed alone in a snow church. I went further afield, I went south and east. I swam in shoals of gaudy fishes, I shared a train compartment at night with escaping reform-school boys, I saw flocks of flamingos at the side of a lake as large as a sea, I climbed a dormant volcano in Java at dead of night, alone. Always alone.

Always I go by air. I am touched, stroked, each time I go through security, my brooch in my pocket.

I have had enough. Each time when I return to the house on its estate, my throat dries in anticipation of a letter, or at least a postcard from Dominic, now surely grown tall and independent. Each time there is nothing. My reserves of optimism are used up. My mind has been returning to lark song high above the moor, to the curlew's swooping cry, to swallows jetting over the river. I miss picking wild garlic, sprinkling the flowers on my egg, its yolk as yellow as king cups, and squashing them in a lunchtime sandwich. I miss picking clutches of wool from fences on long walks to put inside my shoes to cushion and moisten chafed heels. I miss the whine of a wooden kissing gate opening, and the birds singing, morning and evening.

I shall return to the songs and smells.

Tomorrow.